# HORROR OF THE BLOOD DEVILS

# HORROR OF THE BLOOD DEVILS

## TIM CURRAN

Bloody Bones Horror #1
Weird House Press Trade Paperback Edition © 2023

ISBN: 978-1-957121-57-4

Horrors of the Blood Devils © 2023 by Tim Curran

Cover Artwork © 2023, by Michael Squid

Interior and cover design by Cyrusfiction Productions

Editor and Publisher, Joe Morey

Bloody Bones Horror
An imprint of
Weird House Press
Central Point, OR 97502
www.weirdhousepress.com

# Contents

# ONE:
# THE DAMNED

*Pavuvu Island, 1943*

**B**lood.
It was on the leaves and sprayed over the foliage.
It smelled like hot metal and cool pain.

Dog, desperate and dangerous, separated from his unit, moved through the jungle with his Thompson submachine gun held out before him, finger just teasing the trigger. It was nearly dawn and the jungle was cool and damp, seething with pockets of wet mist that danced around him like graveyard phantoms. Knife-edged shadows fell over the thin, rutted trail and above, the sky had gone to indigo, the world delicately balanced between light and darkness. Grainy, dim, but if you tracked men for a living, it was enough.

He crouched down, wiping beads of sweat from his filth-encrusted face, adjusting his Raider cap. A pink worm of a tongue played over his lips, across even white teeth. He knew if he worked his way east, he would reach the Choi River … but there was also a very good chance of running into a reinforced Japanese patrol. He had to be careful now. The enemy knew the Marines had landed. They would be actively hunting them.

Dog had been part of a reconnaissance platoon probing deep into the jungle in search of enemy base camps. It had been a long, dark night, moving along the Choi through the muddy water, tangled roots, and heavy undergrowth. The native scouts had shown the Raiders how to use bits of rotting, luminescent matter from the banks of the river to mark their backs with so they could follow each other in the dark and not get lost.

It was a handy trick.

But somehow, they'd walked right into the middle of a well-entrenched Japanese garrison and all hell broke loose. The Raiders pulled back to defensible ground, but the Japanese sent up flares to pinpoint them. This was followed by a banzai attack—hundreds of soldiers juiced-up on saki and beer led by sword-waving, absolutely fanatical officers.

After that, it was hard to say what happened. The fighting was close-in and bloody, bodies heaped everywhere, pools of blood on the ground deep enough to swallow your shoes.

Dog didn't know if any of the other Raiders had survived, but he doubted it.

He was in a real fix and he knew it.

But this blood … it intrigued him.

He found a few more drops on a wide fan-leaf. He touched a fingertip to it. Sticky, slightly warm. It was recent. But was it the blood of a Jap or an American?

He kept going.

A hole had been punched through the jungle like something big had passed through there, something unconcerned about the trail it had left. Branches were snapped off. Ferns flattened. Vines sheered clean through.

Dog thought: *No pro would leave a trail like this. Whoever did it was either green or stupid or both.*

Of course, there was another possibility, wasn't there? Someone arrogant enough to have no fear of being followed. There was always that.

He saw more blood and marks in the mud like something had been dragged through there roughly, in a hurry. And what might have been footprints, but they were obscured in the muck, just shapeless depressions filling with slimy water.

He continued on, his heart thudding now, his eyes wide. All his senses were tuned to an almost supernatural level and he could hear water dripping up in the trees, hear the flutter of insect wings, the sound of snakes sliding through the undergrowth.

He found a helmet in the bushes. American piss pot. The brim was wet with blood. He had no doubt that it had belonged to one of the Raiders. The Japs must have taken some prisoners and were dragging them through the jungle to a makeshift POW compound.

That was it then.

Did he worry about himself and get out of there, make for the beach miles in the distance or did he go after the enemy? Being that a Marine never left a Marine behind, he knew the answer to that. He had been trained for one thing and that was to kill the enemy in numbers. Here was his chance—yet again. He took a quick inventory. He had two spare magazines for the Thompson, four grenades left, his .45 Colt, a bayonet, stiletto and Marine bowie knife.

He could do plenty of killing if it came to it.

He started to move again, placing each foot down carefully. The jungle was still hazy with night fog and though he could see very well in the dark, there were some things he could not see. The sun would be up soon, but in the triple-canopied jungle, it never got much lighter than twilight. There were always places for the enemy to hide in that primal, mist-haunted soup.

He froze up and went low. *Sounds.* Ahead, he could hear branches breaking and underbrush snapping. Something was out there, something big. He sucked in a thin breath and waited. A man wouldn't make a sound like that. He didn't think so anyway. He felt a white-hot stab of fear in his belly and wondered if it was men he was afraid of or something worse.

Whatever it had been, it was gone now.

His breath hot in his lungs and something cold crawling over his arms, Dog broke into a small clearing ringed by banyan trees strung with looping stranglers and sheets of moss like worm-eaten shrouds hanging from tangled limbs.

Facedown in the mud was a body.

An American.

Dog approached it slowly, listening, watching, waiting for any telltale signs of an impending ambush. Sometimes the Japanese would do that. Leave a rear-guard element to harass and slow-down anyone that was pursuing the main force unit.

But it was clear this time and he slipped from the jungle silently like a monkey and went to the body. He didn't touch it right away, knowing it might be booby-trapped. He checked for wires or sticks or grenades and saw none.

The body had been mutilated.

Left arm ripped off at the elbow. Right leg snapped, the femur thrusting through the flesh like a jagged broomstick. There were deep ruts torn just below the shoulder blades as if somebody had worked a bayonet there. He flipped the body over and saw that the skin had been peeled from the face like the rind of an orange. It looked like a bloody skull. The throat was torn out.

Dog crouched there, breathing hard.

If this was Burma, he'd have thought a tiger had done it. One of the big ones you heard about that routinely devoured both soldiers and peasants alike. They were real monsters. Some of them 600 pounds or more, real primeval monsters that developed a taste for human flesh unless they were put down.

But there was nothing on Pavuvu but some wild pigs.

*Something did this. Something powerful.*

He heard nothing but his own shallow breathing.

The jungle was oddly quiet, the atmosphere tense. Dog waited, dappled by shadow, listening, but not knowing exactly what he was listening *for*. He heard something far ahead—a strange whirring hum

4

like the wings of some gigantic locust. The flesh of his groin began to creep, moving in waves right up to his lower belly. His skin went tight and tingling. His mouth was dry as coal dust.

He was scared. Christ, yes, he was scared.

But it was a different sort of fear, a fear of the unknown, a fear of facing an enemy unlike any he'd known before. Once, on Guadalcanal, he had spent a week ducking in the bush with his platoon while Japanese soldiers hunted him through the hills. He'd been afraid that time, but not like this.

He couldn't put a finger on what exactly he was afraid of this time, but it was bad and it made his guts twist up sickly.

The body before him was still warm, but there was no blood around it. Some soaked into the fatigues, yes, but there should have been a pool around it with wounds like that. It didn't make sense. What he'd found in the brush wasn't enough to explain it.

On a hunch, he took hold of the body by the ankles, hoisting it up until it was in a vertical line. With the throat ripped out like that, blood should've run from the wound, but not so much as a drop came out. He gently lowered it back into the muck.

Animals would claw and bite up their kills, but they sure as hell didn't suck the blood from them.

Dog sat there thinking wild, improbable things.

Bled white.

*Drained dry, drained goddamned dry.*

What he was thinking was insanity, but he thought it nonetheless. In a tight, green world of combat and landmines and body counts, he was allowing himself to be led like a child down a dark path into some fathomless wood. And like a child, his brain was filled with clutching bogeymen and whispering shadows and leering things with white faces pressed to midnight windows.

He shook it away.

Nonsense, that's what. He wouldn't allow such thoughts. He was a realistic man in a realistic world who waded through corpses on a daily basis, looking the ultimate reality of death straight-on in the eye. And death had no room for fairy tales: it was the supreme pragmatist and if there was any evil in the world it had taken the form of men, flesh and blood men with murder, greed, and political agendas in their dark beating hearts.

Dog went down in the mud as noises erupted around him.

Movement.

Stealthy, measured.

There was a thundering sound as something broke from the congested bamboo thicket behind him. He rolled over, bringing up his Thompson. There was a blur of motion and something huge flew over him. If it was a bird, then it was the mother of all birds. A black, nebulous form passing over him incredibly fast and vanishing into the treetops. He was aware mainly of the shadow it cast over him—black and terrible, bringing with it a freezing cold that made the breath frost from his lips.

Then it was gone.

But the air was redolent with its stink, an almost palpable odor of putrescence.

He waited, his arms quivering with gooseflesh.

There was a scream in the distance.

Twisted-up, an echo of agony and horror.

Feeling like he no longer had a choice, he went after it.

-2-

The screams came again.

They reverberated in a shrill wailing through the mortuary stillness of the jungle, broken up and seeming to come from a dozen different directions at once before fading. They were followed by a pathetic voice crying for mercy: *"Oh dear Christ no PLEASE DON'T TOUCH ME DON'T TOUCH ME—"*

This was immediately followed by a wild, weird cackling sound, somewhere between the howl of an animal and the insane laughter of a man. It echoed through the jungle and was gone.

Dog waited. He was after something unusual and possibly unnatural. There was no doubt of it now. A bead of sweat rolled down his face and it was cold as ice.

He moved through the clutching, knotted forest, easing around trailing vines and over rotted trees, through a profusion of ferns that came up to his chest. Blood was sprayed everywhere in loops and droplets. Some of it dripped down on him from high above. And maybe there was a connection to be made there, but he would not allow his brain to make it.

There wasn't time.

He tuned his mind down low, focused it like a beam of light. Concerned himself only with the instinctive act of hunting, of tracking, using all his senses to bring him closer to this thing that hunted men.

He slipped around a deadfall and carefully picked his way down into a verdant, lush hollow that seethed with fingers of mist like tendrils of vapor from a simmering stew pot. He smelled that fetid odor again—high, hot, and suffocating.

He saw movement ahead and went after it.

He caught a glimpse of a body hanging upside down and the momentary, fleeting image of something black and satiny like a nightmare wing disappear soundlessly into the mist.

*You can still get out of here,* an inner voice told him. *There's still time before you see something that will haunt you forever.*

But he wasn't backing down.

He had to see it.

He had to know what this was about.

Slowly, quietly, he approached the body. Another American, his face contorted into an agonized mask. Dog knew this guy and it made something pull tight inside him.

*Frisco. It's goddamned Frisco.*

He was a Raider from Dog's platoon, a medic.

He was mutilated like the other one, ankles encircled with a vine and hung from a tree limb ten-feet off the ground. His throat had been slit open with a surgical-looking incision like that of a razor or scalpel. Gashed open from crotch to throat, his stuffing was scattered in all directions, his ribcage shattered, heart torn out.

Like the other, he was white and bloodless.

And in the distance, Dog heard that inhuman laughter again, that nightmare hyena-like braying. It was as if what had made it, was daring him to go any farther.

## -3-

*How many?*

*How many bodies?*

That's what Dog wondered as he moved through the dense, rank vegetation, still following the blood trail like a hound. He knew he was over his head on this one, that now was a good time to back away and let command call the shots on this.

But he couldn't back off.

And it wasn't just payback either, it was curiosity. Plain, simple, possibly morbid, curiosity. Because he had to see this, had to see what waited ahead. Whatever it was, something in him demanded it. All the fighting and killing and night patrols and ambushes, a lifetime of action and nightmares, yet it had not satisfied him. He'd always sought something more, something no man had ever seen or experienced. That's why he'd joined up in the first place, figuring rightly he could not find what he was looking for in Louisiana. So he joined the Marines, volunteered for elite Raider training, always pushing himself to new heights, searching, searching. And now it had finally, ultimately, come full circle. For this—what lay ahead now—was exactly what he had been looking for.

The sort of thing no man could look upon and remained unchanged.

He paused there as clouds of mosquitoes lit around him and gnats scarfed his throat. He pulled two leeches off his legs, smashed them in his fingers and was amazed, as always, how something that seemed to be composed of nothing more than cold grease could actually be alive.

And that made him think of what was ahead ... was it alive?

He started off again, moving very carefully, not afraid of the Japs now, but something much worse. He moved soundlessly, each step of his sodden canvas jungle shoes taken with great care. The ground was uneven and pocketed with muddy holes and thick underbrush, the jungle draped all around him, wet and hot and steaming. Knife-edged fronds cut his face and snaking vines tangled the barrel of his SMG. Gnarled, dead trees jutted from the waterlogged earth and rotting logs were heaped like railroad ties. Everywhere it was green and misting, cut by shadows and rotting undergrowth. A primeval, haunted world.

But the trail was easy to follow.

Blood was spattered everywhere and the farther he penetrated, hot with sweat and chill with fear, he began to find things. A canvas belt. A pair of smashed eyeglasses. A discarded rifle. A jungle shoe. The shredded and bloody remains of a fatigue shirt. Finally, body parts. First a hand. Then a leg caught in the brush. Finally a torso slit open and emptied. A head speared on a tree limb, its eyes gouged out.

A tickle of madness wormed in his brain.

He had a frantic desire to break into hysterical laughter.

He'd seen insanity in that war, looked it dead in the face. Waded through bodies and blood and carnage...but this was all somehow worse because it was not the work of human evil, but something malefic and spiritually deranged. His guts were heaving and roiling like some ship in a high, windy sea and the stink, Jesus, that stink, was horrible, a charnel perfume of putrefying bodies stacked in mass graves. It seemed to make something in him, something *human,* finally wake up and scream, scream at him: *What the fuck are you doing here, you idiot? Make for the beach. Get the hell out.*

But he couldn't.

He just couldn't.

He'd been a bad boy before the war, always in one scrape with the law after another. Always looking for that high he only got when he was stealing and robbing. And that led him to the Marines where he was assured action and finally, the Marine Raiders. The dangerous work gave him the steady high of living on the edge, courting death.

But there had always been something else.

Something that drove him on, one campaign after another.

The need to see something no man had ever seen before.

He'd been looking for this jungle for a long time. They said there was such a thing as the elephant graveyard, a place where the pachyderms went to die, a netherworld of gigantic skulls and masts of bone, and this, this was the human graveyard. A place where the foliage was so thick, so cloistered that even on the sunniest days, it was a profusion of shadows and pooling blackness. The perfect place for a monster from an evil fairy tale to live.

The forest began to open like a cavern.

Like some perfectly rounded tunnel cut through the jungle, green and shadowy and vibrant. It was maybe ten feet wide, eight in height. But perfect, like it had been cultivated and snipped and pruned. A uniform passage cut through the forest and Dog was following it, the ground wet with blood. The walls of the passage were decorated with dangling legs and arms and torsos and heads. Most were pitted with marks like spikes had been driven into them. The moldering draperies of human skins were suspended from twisted limbs. Not those of soldiers now, but native men, women, and children. Many were fresh and fly-covered, kissed by canopies of worms; but others, he saw, had been there decades if not much, much longer. It must have taken hundreds of bodies to create such a slaughterhouse.

But it was no slaughterhouse.

It was no dumping ground where meat and bone were casually and carelessly tossed. Everything here had been arranged with great care. Whoever or whatever had done this was very proud of this place, a winding altar of human trophies hung in that dripping passage like Christmas ornaments.

Dog took it all in, his soul gone to jelly.

He kept walking, something like coagulated grease lodged in his throat. The passage finally ended and led into the mouth of a cave. But as he looked and looked closer, he saw it was no cave. It was too symmetrical.

It was the carcass of some downed airplane, a big one like a Douglas DC-3 airliner. He'd flown on one before the war. He couldn't see much of it because it was tangled in coils of jungle growth and sheets of moss, drooping tree limbs hanging over it. He could make out the mangled, filthy slat of a wing, but the other was missing or just buried in the earth and leafage. It was sheathed in tendrils and vines, its shell rusted orange where it wasn't green with moss and mildew and jungle rot. Tree limbs jutted from the cabin and roof. The rear ramp was open like a mouth into some black underworld, a multitude of knotted, searching roots feeding from it into the moist soil.

Dog was fascinated by it, as if it was the remains of a prehistoric bird.

Whatever sort of plane it was, it had crashed many years before. In the jungle, all it took was a couple years to engulf a plane like this.

He guessed it had been there six or seven years, maybe longer. Something this big crashing would have slit open the jungle like a knife, left a gaping, jagged wound. But as he looked around, he saw the triple canopy overhead had healed, the foliage was clotted, thick and intact. All that was left of the big bird's death throes was that channel cut into the jungle. It was like a laceration that had been left open, not allowed to heal by whatever called the coffin of the plane home.

Dog knew this was it.

He either walked away or——

But he wasn't going to do that.

Not until he saw.

Not until he *really* saw.

Carefully then, he moved up the ramp and the ancient metal groaned under his weight. There was no way that whatever lived in there did not know he was coming.

Inside, it was like a black, hot envelope of decomposition. Like trying to suck breath through a nitrous, damp shroud. Fingers of light made it in, but just barely. Everything was gray and dim and grainy. Huge, gaping holes had been eaten through the floors and bulkheads. Trees grew straight through it and Chambers had to crawl and weave his way through a network of limbs and roots and branches. The walls were knitted with mats of glistening fungus and pockets of bulging toadstools.

Then he found what he knew he must find.

From the skeletal slats of the bulkheads, hooks were set to handle equipment, but hanging from them were bodies, dozens of bodies like beef hanging in a meat freezer. Many were dead, many were not. He saw Marines, peasants, even a couple of Japanese officers. The hooks had been sharpened like tent pegs, the bodies pressed onto them. The hooks were inserted in the meat between the shoulder blades. It would have been extremely painful, but hardly lethal. It would have taken days and days to bleed to death that way.

The floor was littered with husks of bodies that had withered and dropped from the hooks. They reminded him of the leeched corpses of flies that had fallen from a spider's web, dotting a windowsill.

Dog just stood there—amazed, shocked, offended.

One of the Marines was staring at him, very much aware.

The others were insane, just looking blankly into space, their minds gone to mush, overwhelmed by the horror of it all.

Dog, his heart thudding and his throat impossibly dry, made to go to the trooper, to work him off that peg…but then he suddenly became aware of a heavy, noisome stench enveloping him like a cloud. A raw, heady odor unlike the smell of bodies. He heard a whisper of movement, something like a ragged breath pulled through clenched teeth.

He turned and the Thompson was batted from his hands.

He saw a man-sized black shape lunge at him, a hideous face lorded over by eyes just as red as wet, hothouse roses. Then claws ripped ruts into him and forced him down and something like a membranous wing fell over him.

He knew no more.

-4-

Dripping.

Dripping.

A cave-like dripping sound.

Dog opened his eyes, knowing instantly it was not the sound of falling rain or water running from the trees, but his own blood running from the jagged wound between his shoulders and dripping from his shoes. He tried to move and a sword of agony made white dots dance in his brain.

He was hooked with the others.

Just another carcass sandwiched in with the other livestock.

Below, the floor was black with filth and blood. Worms and beetles crawled in it. A spider ran down his cheek and he felt it leave a thread of silk. Some of the others had cocoons spun at their throats, delicate nets of web laid over their faces like veils.

He wanted to scream and howl and mostly he wanted to die, wishing to God he *had* died in one of the numerous firefights he'd been in. Anything was preferable to this. He looked at the other victims hanging there. They were gibbering, drooling, stark raving mad things. But still alive. Some of the others had been drained dry like peach pits. Still others were ashen and thin, near death.

He thought: *Jesus, not like this, not like this—*

And he started to think of what he had been through. The torturous training, the deprivation, the suffering. All to become a Marine Raider. Only the most highly-motivated could make it through that course, could keep going and going, ignoring the pain and fatigue, surviving through one island campaign after another.

He dangled there, thinking these things … and heard movement, a sluggish rustling as if something was dragging itself forward. And then he smelled that awful odor again and saw it.

*Oh, sweet Jesus…*

It scuttled over the floor like a bat, huge leathery wings propelling it forward through the filth and bones and wreckage. It was more bat than human, he saw, as it rose up. It was hairless and gray, its wings diaphanous. He could see arteries and veins in them. Its flesh was fissured and flaking, the bones beneath practically bursting from the skin. It rose up then and Chambers saw that the head was bullet-shaped with a vaguely human face, but flattened and noseless, the lower jaw jutting forth and set with teeth like knitting needles. The skull was exaggerated with too many bony protrusions and hollows.

He wanted to whimper like a child cowering in bed.

A child that had seen the closet door swing open and had gotten a good look at what lived in there. For this was the mother of nightmares, the seed of vampires and ghouls and night-haunters. Something, perhaps, that had infested the world in ancient times, but was now restricted to this seething, dark pocket of jungle.

It had arms and legs, but no hands as such, just immense black claws that gleamed in the scant illumination like daggers. It bounded from body to body, pressing its puckered mouth to their throats and sucking blood. And that sound—like a straw sucking jelly—echoed through Dog's head until he thought he would go mad.

Then it came for him.

And he saw that the creature had a penis, a short thick member standing erect now. It was excited by what it was doing, moved by grotesque rhythms Dog could not even begin to guess at.

Its breath was like burning hair and its tongue was a flap of sandpaper as it licked his face, tasted his throat. He felt a fan of teeth brush his carotid artery and knew it was over and decided he would simply go insane.

It would be easier that way.

But then a sound reverberated from deeper in the plane: a high, whistling noise that made his flesh creep. The creature moved off, shambling, loping, its wings brushing the shattered bulkheads as it departed with a satiny, whispering sound.

This was his chance.

His only chance.

Summoning everything he had, Dog began to draw himself up, tensing his muscles and pulling, pulling as agony that was white-hot and remorseless exploded in his brain. But he could feel that hook moving, tearing through quilts of muscle and blankets of flesh. And about the time he was ready to pass out, he heard it rip free of his back and he fell to the floor, one leg sinking through the rotting deck.

He pulled himself up, knowing he had no time, no time at all.

It would come for him now.

He needed a weapon, something. He began foraging through the corpses on the floor and they came apart like dry, flaking bark in his fingertips. He kept searching and finally saw an abandoned bolt-action M1903 rifle. His fingers just brushed its wooden stock when he felt the thing come up behind him, its claws like living straight razors scraping over his back.

It knocked him down, made to drag him away.

It was just no good.

Dog couldn't get the rifle, but he still had his web belt. His .45 was gone, but his Marine Bowie was still in its sheath. He pulled it, its 9.5" blade gleaming.

The creature let out a guttural, barking sound and flipped Dog onto his back.

Such was its egotism, it could not conceive of him fighting back.

As it fell on him, he brought the Bowie knife up and the creature's own weight skewered it, the blade sliding between the rungs of its ribs. It went rigid, spraying him with an inky jet of blood, squealing like a rat. It flopped and fought and shrieked and threw itself in circles, firmly impaled. Then it crashed earthward, the rusted deck plating giving way beneath it and it hung there, trapped by jagged shards of metal.

Dog grabbed the M1903 and put the barrel up to its degenerate face.

It snarled at him.

He jerked the trigger, the .30-06 round at close quarters blowing its skull apart, brains and bone fragments sprayed against the hanging bodies and the thing quivered and went still.

But Dog knew there was something else farther back.

He dragged himself forward, the roof overhead open in too many places, wan light spilling in. The sun was up. He found more bodies, piled equipment stripped from them. Carbines. Semi-autos. .45s. Knives. Packs. Boots. Grenades.

Jesus, how long had this been going on?

In the cockpit, he found the nest.

The one he had killed was a male and now here was the female, smaller and bonier, its flesh more white and pink than gray. A mane of hair like a mohawk sprouted from her skull and trailed down the jutting vertebrae of her back. She fixed him with luminous red eyes, giving him a look of complete, relentless hatred. There was a triple set of pendulous teats from her chest to her belly, five or six young—blind and pink and larval—squirmed in the folds of her wings, licking at the foul milk.

The body of a Japanese soldier was hung from the ceiling.

A dozen newborn were attached to it like leeches, sucking it dry.

The young inched toward him like worms.

And Dog brought up the M1903 in sweaty, filthy hands, working the bolt and pulling the trigger. Nothing. Jammed. *Shit.* The female's wings rose up like kites and she hopped forward with a furtive susurration.

Dog screamed and ran.

He thundered through the shell of the plane, bouncing off bulkheads and falling over seats rotted down to the metal frames. He slammed into the hanging bodies and they began to sway like sides of beef in a meat locker. One of them came apart in his fingers like candied glass it was so aged and desiccated.

He could feel the hot breath of the female at his heels, feel her getting closer, hissing and whispering and breathing. And then he tripped over something and rolled down the ramp into the quasi-illumination of the day. A few sickly fingers of sunlight made it through and that was enough.

Enough to stop her.

But he could see her in there, her red eyes glistening like wet blood. He found his feet, ignored the agony threading through him. He stumbled off down the tunnel through the jungle. Two awful days later, bleeding and scratched and insect-ravaged, his jungle fatigues black with filth and dried blood, a Marine patrol found him.

It was some time before he was able to talk and when he told his story, he was sent to Hawaii, a head case. Nobody would believe him and, after a time, he didn't even believe himself.

# TWO:
# THE SWAMP

## -1-

### *Despair Island, Louisiana, 1962*

They were over the wall and across the field before the siren went off and the prison exploded with light—four desperate men in state stripes.

Gus ran with the others, Drake right behind him, shoving him along if he didn't move fast enough. The others, Swede and Carnie, were stumbling along, their legs reaching out for freedom, their lungs filled with good, clean air.

*We won't make it. There's no way we'll make it.*

Gus turned his head and looked back at the high gray walls of Stackhouse Correctional. The gates, the blockhouses, the towers—all of it was lit in a yellow-white surreal glow of sweeping searchlights and security lamps. With the damp, heavy fog rolling in off the Gulf, it looked ghostly, Gothic, a burning city in a black sea of night.

"Move it, shithead," Drake told him, giving him a good shove that nearly planted him to the earth. "If I want you to slow down, I'll tell you."

"Yeah, yeah."

He could feel Drake sneering at him in the dimness. Had they been back behind those walls, out in the yard, he would have beaten him down. Drake didn't take shit from anyone and especially not Gus. He was always looking for a reason to hurt him. If it hadn't have been for Pegg—

"Move it!" Drake told him.

Gus did, dodging across a gravel road and cutting through the pastures of the prison farm. The corn was tall. It smelled green and wet. Drake directed him forward and he ran full out between the rows, the moon high above peeking out from the misty sky now and again like a winking eye. The sirens were screaming, sounding louder all the time. It was this more than the fear of Drake that made him really pour it on like he was heading into the end zone with a ball tucked under his arm.

Sweating and gasping for breath, he broke free of the corn finally and stumbled through short, wiry grasses. The ground was uneven and rough, full of dips and little hollows. He leapfrogged a rotting tree trunk and heard Drake cry out as he tripped over it and hit the ground face-first.

The others hoisted him up and Gus hoped Drake didn't see the smile on his face.

Looking back at the prison over his shoulder as he stumbled and ran through the tangled undergrowth with the others, Gus could almost believe that none of it was real. A dream. A nightmare, maybe, but certainly not reality. It was a scene from a movie. Any second now he was going to see spiking flashlight beams coming at them from every direction.

He climbed over a low wooden fence with the others and jumped into another field. The grasses were high and yellow. It was a real bonehead play but none of them seemed to realize it. They would leave easily discernable trails through the high, dry grasses that would be simple to follow. But nobody asked him and he didn't dare mention the fact. Drake was doing the thinking, Carnie and Swede at his side like lieutenants, and all of them doing what he said just as Pegg had planned it out.

*God, I hope Pegg is out there waiting for us. If we can hook up with him, we might stand a chance.*

Other than Carnie, Pegg was the only guy in Stackhouse that Gus really liked. Pegg was a veteran convict sitting on thirty years for bank robbery. He'd spent most of his life in one hard time joint after the other, reform schools as a kid then state prisons and federal pens after that. He was a thief and he couldn't help himself. He stole cars and hijacked trucks, peeled safes and strong-armed it with banks and armored cars. He was tough and mean if you crossed him so nobody did. A guy like him, a career criminal with a sheet longer than your left arm, had instant respect in any joint he walked into. When he took a shine to Gus, Gus didn't like it. He figured Pegg was after something. Maybe he wanted to extort him or get into his asshole like some of the others, but it wasn't that way at all.

"You remind me of me before I was in the war: a stupid, naïve kid," Pegg told him. "I'm going to straighten you out. I'm gonna see that this is your last time inside. I'm gonna keep all the greasers and perverts away from you. You ain't gonna get stabbed or beaten or raped. Not on my watch, kid. But you're gonna do me a favor. You're gonna keep your nose clean and when you walk out of here, you're gonna be a good boy and do what society says and make something of yourself. That's what you're gonna do."

Gus wasn't about to argue with a setup like that.

He'd only been in two weeks on a manslaughter rap and already the cons were sniffing around him. Drake was one of them. He had randy plans to make Gus his boy. When Pegg found out about that, he took Drake aside. "He's with me. You touch him, they'll find you in your rack with your balls in your mouth. You get me?"

"Sure, sure. What's yours is yours," Drake said.

He didn't like it much, but he knew how the game was played: you didn't poach on another con's turf. You did and you were going to bleed. So even though he was a born and bred thug and bully doing a dime for aggravated assault with prior convictions for attempted murder and rape, he just tucked his tail between his legs and played it cool. But when he looked at Gus, it was right there in his eyes. *Someday Pegg might not be here to protect you, fish. When that day comes, I'll own you and I'll fucking break you.*

Thinking about it now, Gus knew he was really in the shit if Pegg didn't meet them up ahead. The only way out would be to degrade himself as Drake's boy or to kill him. There could be no in-between.

Not with Drake.

He was a predator.

He'd already murdered a guard to get them this far and he wouldn't let anything stand in his way.

The wail of the siren shrieked in the night with a sharp, resounding drone and Gus swallowed down hard. It sounded like the primeval roar of some nameless beast trapped in a tar pit.

Already he could hear the dogs. Yapping. Barking.

*Trained to kill,* Swede had once confided to him in the dull flicker of a homemade candle, his craggy face a shadowy moonscape. *Sure as shit stinks, they train them bastards to kill. Train 'em to go for the vitals. Belly, throat, balls. What does the state care? A couple escaped cons have been accounted for. The books balanced. The public is happy. Safe, warm. What's the difference if some low-life scumbag convict gets his throat ripped out or his balls chewed off? The hacks'll just let them dogs worry a man to death when they corner him. Chomp him up like jerky. Hacks do shit like that. That's why there ain't much difference between them and us when you come right down to it. They're animals and we're animals. We're just on opposite sides of the bars is all.*

That's what was really getting to Gus.

Granted, his plate was full with worrying about being shot down like a crazy dog or getting caught and having his sentence in that rat-infested hole doubled.

But the hounds…

Jesus, those hounds.

If he thought about it and he was really, really trying not to, he could almost imagine the feel of those snapping jaws when they got you. And he could see the guards, too. Sadists like McClaren. Built like a stud bull, his head the shape of a pickle jar, McClaren was dirt mean and got his only real enjoyment in life beating the inmates. It was illegal as hell, of course. But who were you going to tell? The only ones old Mac left alone were the hard-timers and lifers who were just as crazy as he was.

Gus could just envision Mac and his bully boys cornering him against the gnarled trunk of some ancient cyprus tree. Their lights in his face, blinding him. The moon glinting off the barrels of their shotguns and semi-autos. And the hounds straining at the leash to get at him. And old Mac's grinning face as he told the dog handler to let the hounds loose.

They would leap on him like he was a rabbit, claws digging in, sharp teeth piercing his legs and groin and belly, foul meat-smelling breath in his face. He'd scream and scream as his own blood misted in the air and the hounds filled their bellies and the guards laughed with banshee wails—

"Are you with us or what, numb nuts?"

Gus snapped back to reality. Drake's face was inches from his own, sweat beads rolling down it. He could smell his hot, sour breath and see bits of light reflected off the metal studs in his jaw where his uppers should have been.

"Yeah, sure."

"You're lagging behind. What did I tell you about that?"

"Sorry."

"Just keep up."

Gus swallowed down a pocket of damp air because there was nothing else to swallow. His mouth was dry, his tongue like a leather strop. The heat, even at that hour of the night, was unbearable.

*Better watch it,* he told himself. *You better watch it.*

Because Drake had already told him what would happen if he didn't.

## -2-

About the time they were over the wall, Pegg was already nearly two miles away, leaning against a gum tree in the dark and pulling off his cigarette. He had it cupped in his hand the way they'd taught him in the Marines when he was nineteen. That way, the enemy couldn't see the light of your cherry.

Funny.

It was all so funny.

By the time he joined the Corps, he already had two stretches in reform school and juvie prison. They caught him with a hot car—a real sharp '39 DeSoto that would have brought some good change—and gave him six months for grand theft. Despite his record, they went easy on him. But the judge wasn't screwing around. He told Pegg to think very seriously about changing his life before it was too late. The service was the place for a guy like him. The war was raging and the country needed men. The Navy wouldn't touch him and neither would the Army. But the Marines needed boys so, soon as he got out, he signed up and it was off to Parris Island for boot camp. Six months later, he was with the 1st Marine Raider Battalion at the Battle of Bloody Ridge in Guadalcanal.

Two weeks after he was discharged, he robbed a liquor store in San Diego and there had been no stopping him since.

He pulled up the sleeve of his prison stripes and checked the luminous dial of his watch.

Almost 12:30 A.M.

*They should be on their way now. If they hustle, they'll make it by one at the latest. And I'm not about to wait much longer.*

As he finished his cigarette, he heard the siren go off. It made him tense instantly. Dammit. If they followed the plan, they should have been out long before the siren sounded. Pegg began to worry. Something was wrong here. It was all timed to the minute. He went at 11:30, they were supposed to follow at midnight. Something must have happened. Drake must have fucked it up. He should have known better than to trust that idiot with anything that resembled thinking.

*If he gets the kid killed, I'll cut his fucking throat.*

That's what bothered Pegg the most: the kid. Gus had become like a son to him. He couldn't bear the idea of him getting hurt. He hadn't wanted the kid to come, but Gus had overheard Drake and Swede talking about it. He heard the whole thing. There was no choice then; he had to go over the wall with the others. The bulls started sweating him and he would have spilled it all, dropped a dime on all of them without even knowing he had. The kid wasn't tough. He was just a kid. Stupid, dopy, loveable, too innocent for a hole like Stackhouse. He was inside because he fucked up. Pegg wanted to steer him straight. Something that was going to be a lot more difficult now.

*But you had it worked out. The kid could've had a fresh start down in Brazil. You would have seen to that.*

Pegg just waited there in the darkness, wanting to explode out of his skin. The smart thing, he knew, was to run.

He'd had the whole thing planned out, too. He and the others would cut west, get out into the water beyond Sandy Point where the old man would pick them up in the shrimp boat. After that, it would be easy. Once they were out in the big bay, the old man would drop his trawl and Pegg and the others would be down there on the line, twenty feet down in SCUBA gear. Two hours later, they'd be out in the ocean and the old man would bring them up. Then they'd rendezvous with a Panamanian tub which would drop them off the coast of Mexico in a rubber boat. Pegg had a contact in Veracruz, who would give them clothes, fake IDs, the works. And enough cash to get him and the kid down to Brazil where he had good friends, very good friends, in Rio as well as half a million in securities waiting for him under another identity. It was all worked out. It had taken five years to throw it together piecemeal, but now was the time.

Except he couldn't leave.

Not until he knew the kid was okay.

*Even if he stays behind and pulls his time, that would be okay. He doesn't know about Rio any more than Drake and Swede and Carnie do. But if something happened to him—*

If something happened to him, Drake and Carnie and even old Swede were going to wish the hogs had shot them down. Pegg would take his time with them.

-3-

There were three groups out hunting the escapees, a combined force of eighteen men. By morning, there'd be fifty and close to a hundred by mid-afternoon. And by then, every possible escape route on Despair Island would be accounted for. The Coasties would be patrolling the bay, the shoreline watched, every road and dirt trail blocked. And if they didn't have them by then, it would mean they got off the island. And if that was the case, chances were slim that they'd get them at all. At least not for weeks if not months.

The only place on Despair they could conceivably hole up was Snakebit Swamp, a dismal, impenetrable run of reed marshes and black, primeval forest that covered the entire western half of the island, some twelve or thirteen square miles. And if they went in there, they wouldn't be coming out alive. No one ever did. Lots of cons had been lost in that hell zone.

Underwood was thinking it over, wondering, worrying. He'd been a guard at Stackhouse for twenty-seven years now. He knew funny things happened on the island. The kind of things that just didn't happen other places and particularly not to escaped shitheads.

*How many now since you've been here?* he wondered. *How goddamned many vanished into thin air?*

But it wasn't something he liked to think about.

Regardless, he remembered those three narcotics traffickers that went over the wall one night fifteen years before. The dogs tracked them right down to the edge of the Snakebit and that was it. Their trail stopped cold. The warden told the papers and the BOP, the Bureau of Prisons, that they either drowned in the bay or got lost in the marshes and sucked down into the mud. There was an old timer at Stackhouse back then, name of Bobby Steppek. He'd been a guard there since just after World War One. He took Underwood aside one night when they were in the tower and said, *Sometimes they just drop outta sight on Despair. Don't try and figure it or you'll lose sleep. Despair ain't like other places, son. These boys get lost out in the Snakebit and nobody sees 'em again. That's all there is*

Tim Curran

*to it.* Underwood asked him if it was snakes, like the name implied. But Steppek just shook his head. *Worse things than cottonmouths out in those swamps.* Underwood got a chill down his spine remembering that. He'd thought old Bobby had a feather up his ass—one of his ma's favorite sayings when things didn't jibe too good—but he didn't say so. Not at the time. Later, he knew better than to question any of it.

He was waiting there by the gravel road while the dogs casted for scent. It wouldn't take them long. Every second lost enraged McClaren, so Underwood and the others stayed out of his way while he paced about, huffing and puffing like the big bad wolf. The escape had been on his watch. He didn't like that. In fact, it pissed him off to no end. He was the lieutenant of the guard on the graveyard shift and the responsibility was his. It wouldn't look good on his record and he knew it, especially since Danny Clayton was killed. Making captain, something which had been in easy reach these past few years, was now slipping away from him inch by inch.

His group was the only one with dogs. He wanted desperately to bring Pegg and the others in. Especially Drake because he was certain that Drake had done Clayton. Carnie could have done it, sure, and Pegg was more than capable, but neither of them were psychopaths. When they hurt someone it was because of a grudge or someone not showing them respect. Same went for Swede. And Gus…no, he was just a fish. He didn't belong at a place like Stackhouse. Underwood didn't give a damn how many old ladies he ran down; guys like him just didn't belong in the same cage with the animals in a maximum security lockup.

There was a lot on McClaren's shoulders, a hell of a lot. If the State Police ran down the escapees or one of the sheriff's posses did come morning, it was going to look bad. Very, very bad to the warden and the commissioner at the BOP.

"Well? Jesus H. Christ, do those fucking mutts have noses or not?" McClaren wanted to know.

"Easy, Mac," Lofquist said. He was the dog handler. He moved up

27

ahead, leaving Underwood and Peters behind with McClaren to tremble in his bristling shadow.

"Isn't this kind of foolish?" Peters said once Mac was out of earshot.

Underwood shrugged. "How so?"

"Well, listen, Pop, we're on an island here. Where the hell are they going to go?"

"There's places, son. If you're desperate enough."

"You mean the swamps? Those shitheads spend a night out in the Snakebit and they'll be scratching at the gate to get back in."

Underwood just sighed.

*If they knew what was out there, they might at that.*

Mac stomped by them, still huffing and definitely puffing. He was grumbling under his breath. "Leave it to them bastards to run on my shift. Fucking cons. Fucking shitbags. God, but they're going to be sorry when I get my hooks into 'em."

With that, he stomped ahead to lean on Lofquist again.

Underwood had been on four or five of these little midnight jaunts (*rabbit hunts,* Bobby Steppek had called them) and he hoped it ended right here. The smart thing would be to wait for first light. Between the dark and the fog blowing in off the sea, you couldn't see but twenty feet in any direction. They'd never find Pegg and his boys. Not in this. Not unless the dogs treed them like coons.

Stackhouse sat on the east of Despair Island behind high concrete walls. Despair was about two miles out into the Atlantic, a rugged expanse of rock, forested hollows, thicket-covered hills, and fathomless marsh.

"You know," Peters said, "if the warden was smart, if she'd just for once use that piss bucket she calls a head, this could be wrapped up in no time."

"Really?" Underwood said.

Peters stepped into a hole and nearly went down. "Goddammit." He kicked at the uneven ground. "The way I have it figured, we're heading due west, right? Which will takes us—and them—right into those goddamn marshes everyone's so afraid of around here. If the warden was smart, she'd land another group of trackers on the beach by boat. Sooner or later, we'd squeeze our shitheads out. We'd catch 'em right between us."

Underwood nodded. "Sure, that would probably work."

"Damn right it would."

"It would either work or some boys with uniforms and badges would get pulled down into the quicksand out there."

"Shit. Quicksand of all things. Sounds like *Jungle Jim*."

"It's there. Trust me, it's there. You get into the marsh and the grass grows up high over your head and the bog oaks spread their branches so thick you can't see the sky. Chiggers and skeeters so thick they'll drain you dry. Gators out there and snakes and all sorts of crawly things. Sometimes you step on solid ground and sometimes you step into black mud that'll pull you down twenty feet."

Peters just grunted. He wasn't buying it, he just wasn't buying it. That was okay: he was just a kid, a newbie, fresh off his mother's tit. He'd only been at Stackhouse a few years. He didn't know the kind of things that went on there, and particularly out in the Snakebit. Underwood envied him. Ignorance truly was bliss.

A few of the other boys—Charney and Keye—were getting dressed down by Mac. Talking too loud. Old Mac was really on a tear tonight. If he didn't get his shitheads, he was going to make everyone miserable. He wasn't the sort to suffer alone. Guys like him had a habit of spreading the wealth.

He looked over at Lofquist and his dogs, started swearing, then made a beeline for Underwood. Peters immediately wandered off to the others. Underwood stood there, pulling off his cigarette, waiting for it.

"Tell me something, Pop," Mac said, bunching and unbunching his fists, eager for something to strike. "You've been here a long time. How many of these runs you been on? How many times have you done this?"

Underwood took his time in answering. "Four or five, maybe six. Something like that."

Mac chewed that over in his mind. "Some of the boys are saying that none of those cons were ever caught. That true?"

Mac had only been at Stackhouse for the past four years, so he didn't know how things worked. He had the union seniority (and connections) and that got him sergeant right away followed by lieutenant, but that didn't mean he knew shit about how things worked on Despair. Underwood was an old hand. He was one of the few who knew the lay of the land, so to speak. Aside from himself, the old-timers were all gone now.

"It's true and false, Mac. We caught a few, but not many. See, once these guys go over the wall, first place they head is into the Snakebit and that's death at night. Mile after mile after mile of swamp, black water, and sucking black mud holes. One wrong step and down you go. Hanging vines that wrap around your throat, nettles that sting you, bottomless marsh. Gators hiding in the flooded undergrowth and cottonmouths in the water, black widows hanging from the trees. Nasty place by daylight and absolute hell by night. Take my word for it." Underwood took a long, slow pull off his cigarette. His hand shook slightly as he stared off into the darkness. "Can't say how many cons we lost out there. Bones are still there. Only one time, my first year, did one of 'em come back out. And he was struck mad by what he saw."

Mac shook his head and spat into a bush. "Sounds like you're yarning now, Pop."

"Ain't so, Lieutenant. Ain't so. I saw him when he came out. They found him wandering not far from here. A twenty-five year old kid that looked seventy. He was out there a week. His stripes had rotted to rags and his eyes were stark and staring. He saw something that peeled his mind like an apple." Underwood shrugged. "There's things out in that swamp that hunt by night that no man has ever seen. Take my word for it."

"And he was the only one?"

"Yes sir, he was. He went over the wall with four others and we never found 'em. Shit, we lost three good men looking for them."

Underwood could have gone on and on, but it was clear that Mac wasn't believing a word of it. None of it fit in with his view of the world, so he rejected it all. He wouldn't be the first man to make that mistake. Underwood couldn't count on both hands how many convicts vanished out there and how many cops disappeared looking for them.

"That's all ripe bullshit," Mac said, slapping at a mosquito on his neck.

Underwood smiled. "Sweet talk the warden and maybe she'll let you look at the special file she keeps in her safe. It's all in there."

"Special file, my ass."

"It exists, Lieutenant. I've seen it."

Mac shook his head. "You old-timers and your tales." He slapped away another skeeter. "Well, let me give you a dose of reality. What we got out there is just a goddamn swamp with some very desperate shitheads hiding in it and I'm going to get them." He stabbed a finger at Underwood's chest. "And I *will* get them. Mark my words. They belong to me and they won't get away. The only thing that worries me is Pegg."

Underwood ground out his cigarette. "He ain't a bad sort, long as you don't cross him."

"It's what he did in the war that bothers me, Pop. He was a Marine Raider over in the Pacific in the island campaigns. Bougainville, Guadalcanal, all that. Snuck around at night behind the Jap lines slitting throats and blowing ammo dumps. Got himself medals for it, Silver Star, Navy Cross. He was trained to fight and survive in the jungle and swamps. He's the one that might give us trouble, if you know what I mean. A guy like that, sufficiently motivated and trained like he is to operate in that sort of environment, he could be real trouble for my boys."

*He could at that,* Underwood thought. *Might be just the sort of guy who can survive out there.*

Maybe.

And when you factored into the mix that he managed to survive some thirteen years in a violent medieval hellhole like Stackhouse, it certainly tipped the odds in his favor.

"They called him *Dog,*" Underwood said.

"Come again?"

"In the war. The Raiders all had nicknames. They called Pegg *Dog,* on account when he got hold of the scent of the enemy, he never stopped until he ran it to ground."

Mac looked uneasy at the idea.

"Now, you ain't asking for my advice, Lieutenant, but I'm giving it anyway."

"You always do."

Underwood nodded. "You better think long and hard before you send men into the Snakebit at night. Right now, we got us five missing shitheads. You send us in there, you might be light more than a few guards come morning."

"You let me worry about that."

He stomped off, giving Lofquist and his dogs a piece of his mind. Underwood sighed. Mac was bullheaded. You couldn't talk sense to a man like that. He wanted captain and he was willing to do anything it took to get it, regardless of the body count.

-4-

Drake took the lead. He pushed them along, trying to skirt the marshes like Pegg had told him so they didn't get caught up in there, stranded in the muck. Pegg told them that would be their end and Drake was following his orders because Pegg had a good head on his shoulders. They were looking for the big bog oak that was split by lightning into a V years back. That was where Pegg had crossed into the Snakebit. There was a trail in there and if they followed it, it would bring them right to him.

Thinking and planning didn't come real natural to a guy like Drake anymore than it did to most cons. If it had, they wouldn't have been behind bars. That was a fact. So he let Pegg do the mental work.

Gus was right behind him, Swede and Carney taking up the rear. The heat was boiling the sweat out of him and already his prison stripes were soaking wet. It would be worse once they got into the depths of the Snakebit.

*Where we'll probably get lost,* Gus thought. He didn't care much for Drake leading the party. Guy was soft in the head. Sharpening pencils challenged that ball of suet he called a brain, let alone something like this.

Drake was like most hard-timers: completely merciless, utterly ruthless. He was a killer who had been a real terror on the streets. In one lockup after another, he continued that tradition—extorting others cons, beating them, shanking them, piping them. He was an animal and he acted like one. If there was anything human in his skin, Gus had yet to see it.

Swede was okay for the most part.

Once upon a time he'd been a farmer. Then he caught his wife in bed with another man, lost his mind and killed them both with a shotgun. Then he ran. He led the cops on a merry chase across three states, robbing to stay alive, pulling one job after another. Then he hit a gas station and one of the customers happened to be an FBI agent who put three bullets into him. That ended his criminal career. Once he was out of the hospital, he waved a jury trial and pled guilty. They gave him twenty-five to life for first-degree murder and armed robbery. He barely escaped the chair. He'd been behind the walls for fifteen years by that point, most of the hardworking, noble farmer erased from him. He was friendly, easy-going ... but desperate and dangerous when cornered.

And Carnie? Carnie was okay. He was doing twenty years for drug trafficking, second offense. He was a quiet sort. Rarely said anything. He never complained, never bitched or caused trouble, but Gus had heard that if he was pushed he could become a real monster.

Carnie and Swede were a lot alike.

Neither of them were natural predators, but they would fight like hell to protect what was theirs. Unlike Drake with his dead, steel-gray eyes. Murder came naturally to him. He enjoyed it. Case in point, when Clayton had caught them outside their cells after lockdown, Drake hadn't tried to overpower him or knock him unconscious so they could get away. No, he'd slit his throat with a homemade knife.

There had been no hesitation.

*Pegg don't show and that's what you're gonna get,* Gus thought as he moved through the night with the others. *He won't do it to your face either. You know how he is. He'll stick that knife in your throat the first time you turn your back on him. He's a fucking animal. And don't look to Carnie or Swede for help. They're just like the others. They've got nothing to lose.*

Swede trailed behind Drake real easy as did Carnie, but Gus kept stumbling. Everywhere there were mudholes and twisted roots and jagged shelves of rock. They had no flashlights, nothing but thin moonlight to guide them as Drake charged forward, circling the marshes.

"Christ," Gus moaned to no one in particular, startled by how loud it sounded every time they pulled their feet from the sucking mud. "They're gonna find us. I know they're gonna find us."

"Shut the fuck up," Drake snarled.

Swede just ignored him. He vaulted a deep, slow-running stream with ease, scrambling through dry cattails on the other side. He did it simply and quickly in imitation of Drake and Carnie followed suit. Gus made to jump and his left foot slipped on the bank and in he went, splashing around violently.

"Goddammit!" he cried out at maximum volume as his legs sank in the muck, drawing him down. "Shit's like quicksand! I can't get out! Swede! Help me!"

Swede kept moving.

Drake jogged down to the stream and grasped a wet handful of Gus's hair. With a swift, economical motion, he yanked him out of the water and slammed him into the grass. Then he slapped him twice across the face, pulling him to his feet. "Get your act together, shitheel. That water was only a few feet deep. Cry out like that again and I cut your balls off."

"It was the mud."

"Fuck the mud."

With that, he dashed away, moving with an almost preternatural silence like a tiger or a panther; a creature confident with its environment and potential.

Gus stood there a moment, drenched with foul water, blood in his mouth. He ran trembling hands through his stringy blonde hair, wincing at the mournful dirge of the prison siren fading in the distance. He shook his body like a rain-soaked dog and went after the advancing forms of the others.

*A killer,* he thought to himself. *Drake ain't nothing but a cold-blooded killer.*

Carnie grabbed him by the arm. "You're fucking up, my friend. You fucking up real bad. You gotta watch it. Watch it real close."

Words of wisdom.

"Listen now," Drake gasped once they were on high ground. "There's the oak. We're going straight through this shit now. It's gonna be rough. From here on in, I ain't waiting for anybody. You keep up or you stay behind."

Gus knew that was directed at him.

"I'm ready," Swede said.

Gus nodded. He could feel Drake's eyes on him in the darkness. Cold, calculating. The eyes of a snake.

"What were you in for, Gus? Refresh my memory."

"Manslaughter," he said.

Drake grinned. "Oh yeah, that's right. You got drunk and ran down an old lady. I keep forgetting what a stand-up guy you are." He started laughing.

Swede did, too.

Carnie never laughed.

They loved to rub it in his face that he wasn't a hardcore piece of shit like them. That was fine. That was just fine. It was something he took pride in. He hadn't wanted any of this. If he hadn't have overheard them, he wouldn't be along at all. And that would have been just fine with him. First chance he got, he was surrendering. He wasn't about to spend the rest of his life looking over his shoulder. And he sure as hell didn't want to be shot down like a mad dog.

A sudden stink filled the air. A cloying, nauseous smell of rank decay.

It was enough to stop them dead.

"God," Swede said. "That smell."

"Fuck it. Keep going," Drake said.

Gus, however, did not like it. It was so complete, so overpowering. It just didn't seem natural to him. What in the hell could give off such a stink?

"That's how it smells out here," Drake said. "Get used to it."

They moved off, four black shadows against the blacker shadows of night. The land sloped down gradually, the grasses rising higher, black thickets pressing in. They could see water ahead, the moonlight shining off it. The humidity seemed to rise, huge droplets of sweat rolling down their faces. Drake sniffed out the path and the others followed along. It cut through a close-packed thicket that bordered pools of misting bog. The water looked black even with the moon reflecting off it. Dark and dangerous. The farther they went, the louder it became out there with night birds crying out and insects buzzing and whirring.

Gus, easily the most miserable of the lot, watched Swede and Drake ford a stagnant stream with little difficulty. Then came his turn. The water was unpleasantly warm like blood. His boots sucked down into the mud. He slipped, tripped, fought, went down and came up drenched and complaining. He could hear Drake's muffled warnings to lower his voice.

But he'd reached the point where he didn't even care.

On the opposite bank, the others waited amongst the low sprawling bushes and congested scrub brush. Gus shambled wetly over to them, his stripes black with mud. There was a sudden movement and stars exploded in his head. He swam from the edge of blackness to find himself sprawled on the spongy loam, blood running freely from his gashed mouth. Drake squatted by him, his features near invisible, but his intent all too obvious.

"What the hell did you do that for?"

Drake clapped him upside the head and lights buzzed fiercely in his head again.

"What do you think?" he said, jabbing a bony finger at Gus's wheezing chest. "Now straighten up, shit-for-brains. Last warning."

Gus said nothing; there was nothing he really *could* say. He would take it because he had no other choice. Sooner or later, the tables would turn. That's how life worked. Sooner or later, Drake would need him and when that time came, that asshole would come up dry and empty-handed.

*Go ahead, leave me here. I'm okay with it,* he thought as he tried to overhear what Swede and Drake were talking about. He had no doubt that it had something to do with him.

"Should I kill him now, Swede? Get it over with?"

"No," Swede said. "Give him one more chance. But just the one."

Gus sensed, rather than saw, a sinister understanding pass between the men. The atmosphere around them seemed to chill noticeably. He knew what was coming; it was only a matter of when.

"Nobody's killing anybody," Carnie said, not bothering to keep his voice low.

"Who fucking asked you?" Drake shouted, trying to menace him but having a hard time of it because he knew how vicious Carnie could be if you cornered him.

"Pegg told us how to do this and we better do it the way he said," Carnie told them. "I wouldn't want to be the one who fucked up his instructions. I wouldn't want to be the one who shanked Gus. Because if you're that man, you're going to die."

Gus waited for Drake to puff out his chest and stomp his feet, go into his prison yard banter about how he feared no one and he was in charge and if he wanted to kill a fish he'd damn well do it. But he didn't say a thing and neither did Swede. They were bad, bad boys, but they were both scared shitless of Pegg and his black moods.

Gus, feeling empowered now, stood up and said, "Well, we gonna sit here all night or what? C'mon, Drake. You want to be the leader then act like one. Lead us the fuck out of here."

Swede chuckled in his throat.

Drake didn't say a thing, but Gus was pretty sure he was thinking plenty. He probably had all kinds of dark little ideas in his head. Until they got to Pegg, Gus decided it probably wasn't a good idea to let Drake get behind him because Pegg or no Pegg, Drake was going to kill him. It was just a matter of when.

-5-

*Well, that was a close goddamn shave,* Carnie thought.

Like a stropped razor at your throat, it could have gone either way. That goddamned kid, goddamn Gus, he just wasn't cut out for this kind of shit. Drake had his number and he wanted to do him real bad, just as he'd wanted to for months now. The only thing that stood in the way of that was Pegg. And the only thing that was standing in his way now was Carnie himself.

*But for how long?* he wondered. *How long can I possibly keep Drake off him?*

That was the big question, of course. Under ordinary circumstances, Carnie knew, he could have counted on Swede standing with him against Drake. Hell, they'd always been tight and had been cellies eight years going on nine. There was an understanding between them.

Unfortunately, all that had changed because these were not ordinary circumstances. Swede had tasted freedom now via Drake and he was desperate to hang onto it. He would kill to safeguard it. And if he had to, he'd join with Drake if that's what needed to happen. Both of them were afraid of Pegg, but Pegg wasn't with them now and that had gotten the gears whirring in Drake's head.

Carnie figured he could handle Drake if it came down to it, but not if Swede came at him, too.

Two days ago, Pegg decided that the kid had to come with them when they went because he had overheard Drake running his mouth about it all.

"I don't like it either," he said, "but we don't have a choice."

"I suppose not."

"He's a good kid, but he'll never stand up to the bulls. You know it. I know it."

Pegg said it would still work out the same. He had copies of the cell keys. He'd unlock his own cell after the guard passed on his rounds, then he'd unlock the others. He'd go first. If he made it out on the route he'd planned, so could they. Thirty minutes later, they'd follow, get over the wall, and make for the V-shaped bog oak. Only difference was that Gus would be coming with them.

"Now I need you to help me on that," Pegg said. "Can I count on you?"

"Sure."

"I'm trusting you to keep an eye on him. Drake is just a dumb animal and Swede ain't much better. You got a brain and you got heart. Watch over the kid until you meet up with me. Can I trust you to do that?"

"Absolutely."

Pegg had been good to him through the years. Anytime he got in a beef with another con, Pegg had always been there to back him up. They'd fought side by side with lead pipes and shivs in their hands more than once. And Carnie would never forget the time he'd gotten into it with that psychopath bayou trash Slim Pickapaw. Slim had planned on killing him in the machine shop and Pegg had found out and intervened. Old Slim had it all worked out—he and some of his heavy-hitters arranged to get Carnie alone. But what they hadn't counted on was Pegg. He came out from behind the lathe with a four-inch, double-edged shank with duct tape wrapped around the handle.

And quiet, too.

Just as silent as a rat snake from a mouse hole.

Slim's boys ran, because they didn't want any part of Pegg. But not Slim himself. He'd had about enough time to gasp as Pegg slapped a hand over his mouth from behind, yanked his head back, and drove three-inches of cold steel into his brain pan via the soft tissue under his right ear. Slim hit the ground, convulsing. Then he went still as a dead river cat, blood seeping from his ears and eyes.

"I owe you," Carnie said.

"Nothing to it," Pegg told him. "An old Raider quick-kill technique.

I greased a dozen Jap sentries that way during the war. We never mention it again."

So, Carnie owed him and he was loyal to him. He'd die protecting the kid if he had to.

The idea of that, of course, sounded a lot easier back in the prison than it did out here. The Snakebit was like a prehistoric swamp by moonlight—primeval, menacing. The bald cypresses and bog oaks hanging with vines and Spanish Moss. Unseen things splashing about in the shadows and undergrowth. Snakes sliding across black pools and big gators floating like logs in the flooded, reedy channels. The grass out here was tall as a man, the skeeters and gnats and chiggers thick as mist. Leeches dropped from the trees and nameless things cried out from the sucking black depths.

It was all bad enough without Drake and Swede, goddamn Gus fucking up at every turn and pissing them off. Carnie knew he was going to be damn lucky if he delivered the kid to Pegg unscathed.

But he would do it.

Someway, somehow, he'd do it.

Poor, stupid kid. What had the courts been thinking putting a dumb little puppy like him in a cage like Stackhouse? Carnie moved forward, watching not only the kid but Drake and Swede. It was only a matter of time now before Drake tried something and he had to be ready.

-6-

The feeling in Pegg's gut that something was terribly wrong or about to become so increased. He tried to talk himself out of it but it was no soap. He waited there by the tree, anxiety rising in him. He was worried about the kid. About Swede and particularly Drake, because neither of them were particularly bright. Carney was the only one with a head on his shoulders. But if it came down to it and Drake decided to do the kid, Swede would just stand by and watch. Carnie was his only hope.

*They hurt the kid and I'll—*

The thought ended right there as something big, *very* big, splashed out in the swamps. Tense, he waited. Things scurried in the undergrowth and something droned at his ear. He slapped it away, brushing mosquitoes from his neck.

*What in the hell was that?*

He couldn't figure it. He knew the animals that should be out here and none of them were big enough to make such a sound. He felt fear wash through him, the sort of fear he hadn't felt since Bougainville when you could hear the big crocodiles moving around you in the swamps at night. No crocs out here, though. A few gators, but nothing gigantic. And that had surely been a gigantic sound.

He stepped away from the gum tree, peering through the brush at a labyrinth of ponds in the moonlight. They stretched endlessly, bald cypress trees rising up from them like the masts of sunken ships. It was quiet out there now. A few minutes before it had been busy with the croaking of carpenter frogs and peepers. Now it was dead silent.

Pegg felt the skin begin to crawl along the nape of his neck, the way it had in the war when he could sense the enemy sneaking up on his position after dark. He was certain something was out there. That he was being watched from the depths of the swamp. He couldn't see anything in the gloom, but that didn't mean it wasn't there. He was a guy who had learned to trust his instincts. He peered close. With all the trees, rotting stumps, and floating logs, it was hard to tell what was out there.

He swallowed, his skin prickling.

Huge beads of sweat rolled down his face.

*If you're there, then show yourself.*

But it wasn't going to be that easy and he knew it. Whatever was out there was very patient. It wasn't a search party. They would have made so much noise you could have heard them on the mainland. And it wasn't Drake and the others because they wouldn't have been much quieter. No, this was something that was very comfortable in about this place. Something that was part of this misting, green primordial world.

Pegg slipped the shank out of his belt. Not quite the Bowie he'd carried in the Marines, but it would do in a pinch. He retreated behind the gum tree. Waited. Watched. A stand-off. Whatever was out there was doing the same thing.

*Ain't you giving it a little too much credit?* he asked himself. *What's out there is an animal, a big one, but it's still an animal.*

Yes, that was realistic ... but sometimes, he knew, when you were in a bad situation in an unfamiliar place, you had to trust your gut-sense and your feelings. And what they were telling him was that what was out there was not only big, but crafty. Maybe not intelligent in the way a man was, but cunning, its instincts sharpened like a knife against a stone.

He felt the shank in his hand. It was sharp, deadly against another man, but worthless against what he was facing. He hadn't been this scared since Pavuvu.

*Stop it,* he told himself. *You remember what they told you in the hospital. You had jungle fever, you were delirious. You never saw what you thought you saw.*

But he didn't believe that. The memories still came back to him in his dreams. The carcass of the plane. The hanging bodies. Those night-shapes feeding on blood.

*That was in the Pacific, not here.*

Sure, something like that couldn't happen here. He had to keep that in mind. Jesus, he had just escaped a max-security lock-up, was it any wonder his nerves were a little frazzled?

This was what he told himself and it sounded good, but at his core, where the wild things were, he did not believe it. His nerves were humming like tuning forks the way they had during the island campaigns and, particularly, Pavuvu. His tongue felt swollen in his mouth, his throat dry. He didn't think he could have uttered a sound even if he wanted to.

It was then that he became aware of a horrendous, black stink of putrescence. It was more than the stink of rotting things in the swamp, the rotten egg sulfur odor of rising methane and decay. This was a pungent stench of death and it was coming from out there, from whatever was hiding itself in the drifting sheets of swamp gas.

He thought for a moment he saw the shine of gleaming eyes.

Shank in hand, he waited for what was out there to show itself, something horrific and night-winged. Then, whatever it was, it was gone. As if evidence of that, the creatures of the swamp began moving again, lowing and chirping and buzzing.

And he was alone.

Alone as he'd been in Pavuvu and that was the thing that made his flesh crawl.

-7-

Sergeant Teague was not in the best of moods. He knew when word reached him that some of the shitheads had escaped that he'd end up leading one of the parties. True to form, McClaren had chosen him and now here they were, out in the Snakebit, huddled in the darkness, waiting for orders while the mosquitoes drained them dry.

"Why don't you get on the horn again, Sarge?" Marco said. "Tell McClaren we're fucking dying out here."

"Shut your yap. He wants us to stay put until he says different."

There was some grumbling over that. Tonight, there'd been a lot of grumbling. The men were dirty, tired, faces scratched by picker bushes, mud right up to their hips. The swamp spread out in all directions, dark and impenetrable. Black gum trees rose from the green-slicked water, the moonlight making them shine with a ghostly phosphorescence.

Marco grunted. He was the last guy Teague wanted in his search party. He was a born complainer that had a way of souring anything he was involved in. Any group he was part of had a way of going to shit with him and his sour grapes. At first, the others ignored him, but after a solid two hours of his bullshit, they were drawing closer to him like he was some kind of sage rather than the crybaby they all knew him to be.

Not that some of his sour grapes weren't justified. This entire situation was bassackwards from the word go. Teague had been a guard at Stackhouse for years now and the one thing you never, ever wanted to do was chase escaped cons into the depths of the Snakebit. Especially at night. But there was no talking sense to McClaren. He had to pull his

*43*

shitheads back in. That was a priority. If he didn't, it would leave an ugly stain on his squeaky, clean record that would never wash clean. And guys with sullied records didn't get promoted.

Teague knew that Underwood and some of the other old hands had tried explaining the danger of the swamp to him, why you never went in there after dark and not even during the day if you could help it. Despair was an island, for god sake. Cover the water around it, patrol the shoreline, and sooner or later, you'd have your boys.

And if those idiots went into the Snakebit, well, the problem would solve itself.

"So, what is it Mac wants us to do out here?" Marco asked. "We got flashlights, we got guns, but that's it. We've got no dogs and a dozen square miles of swamp staring us in the face. How is it we're supposed to track those shitheads?"

Labonski nodded, pulling off his cigarette. "You got a point there, that's for sure."

The others—Wiles, Corbett, and Suterman—grumbled in agreement.

"Listen, goddammit," Teague said. "I'm just following orders, same as you. Mac is in charge. He says wait in the swamp, scratch your asses, and listen for the escapees; well, that's what we do."

"If I see 'em, I'll shoot the sonsofbitches. Killing Danny like that. He was a good kid," Suterman said.

That got them all going. Grumble, grumble, groan.

Teague shut them out and kept his ears open. It was all he could do. He liked Danny Clayton just as much as they did, but he couldn't let emotion cloud his judgement.

They were crouched on a bridge of dry ground that sat above steaming morasses of black water to either side. Out there were floating rafts of reeds, little islands of sawgrass, ferns, and scraggly cedars. Beyond, was open water draining down into the heart of the swamp, a forest of dead trees rising up like monuments.

Now and again, they heard animals splashing out there, the near-constant croaking of frogs and the shrill piping of night birds, what might have been a woodpecker in the distance knocking on the trunk of a tree.

Corbett was monitoring the radio, an Army surplus walkie-talkie, the old AN/PRC-6 that Teague remembered was called a Prick-6 in Korea. Corbett had it pressed to his ear, listening intently for any activity out there. He kept shaking his head, so there couldn't have been any.

"I bet Mac knows exactly where they're hiding," Marco said, "but he sent us out here to make it look good. A full-scale manhunt. He gets his shitheads, we get malaria and leeches. Lucky if one of us don't get chewed up by a gator."

Teague smiled. When they first got out here, something long and snaking had slid from the grass into the water and Wiles had screamed like an eight-year-old girl in a carnival spook house.

"Gator!" he cried. "It's an alligator!"

Labonski laughed. "Ain't no gator. Just a weasel."

"Not so," Marco said. "That was what's known as an ermine."

"Oh, all of you just shut up. It wasn't but a couple feet long," Teague told them.

But that was Wiles, all right—every vine was a water moccasin and every spider web was a nest of black widows. Between his paranoia and Marco's conspiracies, Labonski's griping and the brooding of the others, it was going to be a long goddamn night.

As Teague waited, listening—and he wasn't sure what for—he began to feel tense. He became increasingly apprehensive as if he was expecting something to happen. His throat had gone dry and his muscles were drawn taut. His eyes seemed to be bulging from their sockets and he had to remind himself to blink. He could feel his heart thumping in his chest and his breath was coming fast. It was like … like waiting for a shot, a needle to jab you in the arm. You knew it was coming, but not the precise second.

There was a sudden wheezing, flatulent sound and Wiles said, "What the hell was that?"

45

Labonski and Suterman laughed.

"That was Corbett's ass," Marco said.

"What? Oh, Jesus, I can smell it now."

"I got bad digestion," Corbett explained.

Marco sighed. "See what you got us into, Sarge? We sit out here in this bug-infested hell hole while Corbett shits his pants."

"I ain't never shit my pants ... except that once. And the old lady's bean soup was to blame."

More laughter. But was it Teague's imagination or did it sound more than a little forced? A little fake and tinny as if the men were trying to reassure themselves with good humor, trying to chase away the boogeyman and failing miserably at it.

"Pipe down," he told them.

Wiles said, "Yeah, but—"

"Shut ... up."

Teague meant it now. Something had happened out there in the swamp. It was like a switch had been thrown and everything, night and animals and insects, had gone dead quiet. Nothing moved. Nothing stirred. It was as if a blanket (or a shroud) had dropped over the world.

Beads of sweat that felt big as peas rolled down his face. His jaws were locked tight. His breath would barely come. He could hear the men breathing, feel Wiles trembling inches away. They were all feeling it, knowing something was out there, something unnatural. They had become a closed circuit of terror.

Flashlight beams were spiking in the swamp mist.

"Turn 'em off," he told them. "Right now."

The world went dark.

It reminded him of Korea, the heavy fighting around Hill 255. Those long, dark nights dug in along the ridge, the guy next to you just a vague shadow ... and, suddenly, everything would go still as a graveyard and you knew a gook sapper was sneaking up on your position or a sniper was drawing a bead on you. After a time, you got a sixth sense about it and you knew exactly where they were.

And right then, just inside the doorway of Snakebit Swamp, he felt it again.

Something was out there.

Something was watching them.

He could feel its cold, alien eyes doing the slow crawl up the nape of his neck. And just like during the war, he knew exactly where it was hiding. Beyond the morass of black water, off to the right there was an open pool like a small, misty lake. Dead center of it was a gigantic bald cypress draped with moss.

What was watching them was up in the tree.

"Should … should I get on the radio?" Corbett whispered, so close Teague could feel his hot breath in the cup of his ear.

"Quiet," he told him in a dry, cracking voice. "Don't anybody so much as move … "

Something cracked in the big cypress and a branch splashed into the water. The noise of it echoed on and on through the lowlands.

Then there was a flapping, whooshing sort of sound and they saw it, just for an instant—a black shape with fanning, scythe-like wings. Like a bat, but easily the size of a man. It was there for a split second, soaring against the misty face of the moon as it jumped from the top of the tree.

Then it was gone.

Teague started breathing again, his head spinning so badly from the lack of oxygen he thought he might pass right out.

"Did you … did you fucking see it?" Wiles asked, gasping. "Jesus, did you see it?"

And Marco answered for all of them: "Shut up … for the love of God, just … shut … up…"

## -8-

The swamp, the mud, that was the key. The more Drake thought about it, the more sense it made. Fucking Gus. He hated that little sonofabitch, goddamn fish like him running his mouth and all because he had Pegg's protection. Without him, well, it would have been a different story for him at Stackhouse.

*I'd have broke him and schooled him,* Drake thought. *Oh, Christ, yes, then I would have sold him to one of the old short-eye perverts for a toy.*

The idea made him smile. Fish like Gus weren't good for anything else. They were no good this side of the wall, just punks looking for a daddy to protect them. Pegg had some kind of fucked-up father/son thing going with that little shit. Pegg, of all people. Not that there was anything wrong with him. He always did the right thing. He'd been raised up right behind bars and was the first to throw someone a beating if they disrespected him, first to stand with a friend if they were threatened. Hell, even the hacks liked him. And if they didn't like him, they at least feared him and his violent temper.

But this thing with Gus.

No, Drake didn't like that. He'd seen him first and he had plans for the punk. Then Pegg stepped in as his father-protector.

Well, that bullshit was going to end now.

They'd taken a few wrong turns in the Snakebit and they were behind schedule, but the way Drake had it figured, within thirty minutes, they'd hook up with Pegg, and before that happened, Gus was going to be a dead man.

The problem was going to be Carnie.

He was keeping an eye on him. Somehow, he had to get him away from Gus in the dark, then the rest would be easy. Drake would slit the kid's throat, sink him in a mud hole, and that would be that. He'd act all surprised about it. *Where's the kid? Anybody seen the kid?* They wouldn't have any choice but to move on.

That's how it was going to work.

Drake had it all planned out.

Sure, Pegg would go apeshit, but let him. It wasn't their job to babysit his boy.

The time was coming.

## -9-

"What're you two yabbering about?" Mac asked with his usual venom. "Keep quiet for chrissake. The dogs got something. It's time to make our move."

"You ain't thinking of going out there?" Underwood said.

Mac grinned. "You're damn right I am. We're *all* going out there."

"Warden ain't gonna like it."

"You let me worry about that, Pop."

Off he went and they followed along, keeping quiet, but with the baying of the hounds it didn't seem to much matter. It wasn't like they were going to sneak up on anyone but the deaf and blind. The ground was sloping and damp, pocketed with muddy draws, jutting hillocks, and sudden, ankle-twisting hollows. There were dark stands of pitch pine and denuded birch. Huge, misshapen elms rose up, leafless and black, their crooked, knotty limbs fanning out above like spiderweb tracery. The trackers continued on, led by the anxious dogs, their flashlight beams like white swords in the mist.

They were going into the Snakebit and things were going to get bad. Underwood knew it. But there was no talking to Mac. Just no talking to him. He had an agenda and anyone who didn't get onboard with that was going to lose their job. Mac would see to it.

"Blacker'n the fucking pit," Peters said. "And that stink. You smell it?"

*Just the marshes,* Underwood thought. *All that stagnant water and mud, rotting stumps and sunken trees. Swamp gas.*

He found the idea reassuring even if he didn't really believe it.

"Gone now," Peters said. "That's funny. The smell is gone now."

Whatever Underwood might have said, he kept to himself. No need spooking Peters; he'd get plenty of that on his own now.

The land was sloping down now like the side of a bowl as they entered the lowlands. Underwood could see the heavy undergrowth, thick-boled trees, the moonlight shining off mud holes and ponds. Now they were getting into it.

Every now and then the dogs lost the scent. Somehow, they kept getting turned around, confused, chasing their own tails and doing a lot of growling as if it was all making them angry. Lofquist kept trying to get them under control while they sniffed every blade of grass, every bush. He would lead them in what seemed to be circles, casting for scent. When they found it, they'd nearly pull his arm off in excitement. But every now and then, the hounds would stop dead and start whining, clinging to him as if he were their mother.

"C'mon, damn you!" he bellowed at them. "Afraid of your own goddamn shadows or what?"

When Mac lost his temper and made to kick one of them, Lofquist came right out of his skin. "Don't you dare touch one of my dogs. You hear me?"

"Yeah, yeah. Get them moving."

"You keep in mind one thing, McClaren: they're the only way we're going to find your shitheads and once we get deep in the Snakebit, they're the only thing that'll get us back out again. So mind your manners."

McClaren looked like he was going to cuff him, then he backed down. "Just keep 'em moving. What the hell's wrong with 'em anyway?"

"I don't know. I can't figure it. Never seen 'em act this way before."

"Maybe there's something out here they don't like," Underwood said. "Something that scares them."

"My dogs ain't afraid of nothing."

"Except their own shadows," Mac said.

Peters chuckled.

Lofquist shook his head. "You don't know what you're talking about. You don't know shit about tracking. I'm their handler."

"Then fucking handle them," Mac said.

Swearing under his breath, Lofquist tried to get them under control.

Underwood couldn't help but notice that these little episodes always coincided with that godawful smell. Like maybe the dogs were frightened of it for some reason.

"Christ, enough to make you puke," Peters said.

"And then some."

"You from these parts?" Peters asked. "I mean, you know, the mainland."

Underwood wiped a spray of mist from his face. "Born and bred."

"I heard a group of Caddo Indians once got slaughtered on this island. That true?"

"Hell if I know." Underwood seemed disturbed by the idea. "There's lot of stories about Despair. That's the problem with this part of the country. Too much history. Gets to where history starts crowding the present."

Peters nodded as if he understood all too well, even though he was completely mystified by the idea.

"Shut your yaps," McClaren told them. "This ain't a Boy Scout hoo-ha."

They continued on, boots sinking into the soft earth. They were getting into the marshes proper now. Peters kept slipping and falling, tripping over jutting roots, swearing the entire time. Everywhere there were dark, stagnant pools and steaming bogs. McClaren stuck close to Lofquist. Underwood had the feeling that he had finally come to the realization that he was out of his depth in the Snakebit and was now trusting completely in the man and his dogs.

It sure seemed like Lofquist knew what he was doing. He seemed to know the way, guiding them across narrow grassy slopes, avoiding dips and sinkholes. Peters and Underwood were behind Mac, Charney and Keye trailing them, shining their flashlight beams in every which direction.

"This is bullshit," Peters said after he'd picked himself up for what seemed the hundredth time. "We should just wait for daylight."

Underwood simply nodded, keeping his eyes on the ground.

"You been at Stackhouse, what? Twenty years, Pop?"

"Twenty-seven."

"Shit, you should be lieutenant, not Mac."

He shrugged. "Didn't want it. Sergeant is fine with me. You go above that pay grade and you got to play politics, not to mention the paperwork."

"I guess that makes sense."

"Sure."

"But how many of these you been on in that time? Hunting escaped shitheads?"

Underwood chuckled low in his throat. "I don't know. Five or six. Something like that."

Peters shook his head. "Now that's bullshit. How the hell do these guys keep slipping out?"

"I don't know, but they do. The prison's old, run down. And those boys got nothing better to do twenty-four hours a day than to think of ways to escape."

"In the end, you always get 'em, though. Right?"

Underwood shrugged. "A few. Some we never saw again. But we keep trying. Nobody can say we don't."

"Boy, I like that," Peters said.

Underwood ignored the sarcasm. If they were lucky, they'd come back empty-handed with nothing but muddy boots, wet pants, sore backs, and faces scratched by pickers. That's what he was hoping for. He wasn't so much worried about what they'd find in the marshes but what might find them.

About a half an hour into the trudge, the dogs went wild. They started yapping and howling, snapping at Lofquist and McClaren, huddling together and whining. They were acting not only confused, but frightened. Underwood didn't know a lot about bloodhounds, dogs were dogs to him, but if he didn't know better, he would have sworn they caught the scent of something and it had them scared shitless.

Lofquist tried yelling at them and disciplining them, but it did no good at all. They just got that much more belligerent and hard to control. Finally, he sat with them, gathered them around him, stroking them and whispering to them. That seemed to do the trick after a time. It calmed them.

Meanwhile, Mac had Charney get on the walkie-talkie and make contact with the other search parties. Teague's group had just entered the swamp from their location, but had seen nothing.

"Not getting anything from Millhaus, Lieutenant. I've tried three, four times. Just dead air."

"Probably out of range."

"Probably," Underwood said.

Whatever he meant by that was ignored by Mac. He took the walkie-talkie from Charney and tried himself. He had no more luck.

"It's only good for a mile," Charney said.

"Okay. The dogs are moving. Let's go."

"They got something," Lofquist said. "And they're leading us right to it."

Which was what Underwood worried about. Maybe it was just the shitheads. If that was the case, no harm done. They'd get their escapees, bring them in dead or alive, and this rabbit hunt would be at an end.

And if it wasn't Pegg and the others, well, then things would get interesting.

## -10-

They were late.

They were very late.

And every second counted. That was the thing Pegg had tried to impress upon them, that everything was worked out to a very rigid timetable. They needed to be at the rendezvous point at a certain time, give or take ten minutes, so he could lead them out of the Snakebit to the beach where they would swim out and the old man would pick them up in the shrimp boat. Things were going to be getting hot and the old man wouldn't hang around long. If they missed him, they were done. It was all over.

He checked his watch.

*Shit. Already an hour late.*

Pegg kept telling himself that he couldn't understand why they hadn't made the rendezvous, but down deep he knew. There could only be two reasons—either they'd already been caught already or Drake had fucked it all up as Drake managed to fuck up everything that required anything beyond the most rudimentary thinking. Pegg had gone through it with him dozens of times, drilling it into his head. If he did what he was told to, it should have worked perfectly.

But it hadn't, which meant Drake was to blame.

He was the reason everything was going south. Five years to throw this together and that idiot had wrecked it all in an hour.

That's when Pegg decided he was going to have to kill him. There was no other way. He was a liability.

*That's if he ever shows.*

Pegg knew that they were quickly running out of time. If he moved now, he might still make it out to the shrimp boat … but he couldn't abandon the kid like that. He just couldn't.

He weighed his options.

What it really came down to was that he might have to face the prospect that he was alone. The Snakebit went on forever. Over a dozen square miles of wasteland of the sort he'd been trained to fight in during the war. He figured, if it came down to it, he could hide out in the swamps for months. But he'd need a rifle. Once he had that, he could survive until he figured a way to get across the water to the mainland. And if worse came to worse, he would give the men that hunted him a war like they'd never seen before.

But if it came to that, they'd never stop hunting him.

He checked his watch again.

Fifteen minutes. That's all he could give them, then he had to make his move. He just couldn't wait any longer.

It was quiet out there. He could still hear the siren far in the distance, but no sounds of dogs or men closing in. That was good, anyway. He had a cigarette, cupping it in his hand so it could not be seen. He listened to the wildlife out there and it reminded him so much of all those long nights in the island campaigns that it made him uneasy. His mind turned back to those things it had spent years trying not to remember.

Pavuvu.

*Pavuvu.*

After he'd escaped from the wreck of the plane and the things that used it as their lair—*delirium, hallucination, you didn't really see them, night-things, night-horrors, couldn't have been real*—he'd stumbled blindly through the jungle, out of his mind, broken by terror, injured and sick, getting more and more lost. All day, he'd crawled through the forest, fording streams and crossing rivers and fighting through swamps, getting weaker and weaker. He woke the next morning and he was in a tree. He had no memory of climbing it. His training and instinct had kicked in. The last thing you wanted to do was sleep on the jungle floor. At night, it was a crawling carpet of insects, of centipedes and spiders, ticks and snakes. So he'd climbed into the tree.

He still had his web belt and knife. In one of the pouches, he found some K-Rations: cheese and crackers, some chocolate. He ate them and it cleared his head a bit. But he had no water. It had rained during the night and he drank from a puddle, knowing he was probably infesting himself with all sorts of parasites. But he had little choice.

Taking a fix on the sun, he moved in the direction which he thought would bring him to the beach, but what he found instead was one Japanese patrol after another. Finally, he had to turn back, slipping into the dim confines of the triple-canopied jungle, moving stealthily from one bush to the next. It took a lot out of him and he was in poor shape to begin with. He couldn't move like when he was healthy. He'd make it maybe half a mile, oftentimes less, and then he'd collapse again and sleep.

When night came on again, the terror seized him because he knew what hunted it. Those things that could not go out in the sunlight. He climbed another tree. The rain poured down again and even hidden in the branches, it soaked him to the skin. His fever was bad. He was shaking constantly, his mind more confused than ever. He woke several times, thinking that one of the creatures from the plane was in the tree with him, touching him with its cold claws and sipping blood from his throat.

Toward morning, he had a waking nightmare of them and slashed madly at phantoms with his knife.

He fell from the tree into the muddy earth.

When the sun came up, he moved again, letting his instincts guide him. Crusted with mud, sweating with fevers, beaten and bruised, cut and scratched and swollen from insect bites, he was found by Marines late that day.

And that's how the war ended for him.

It was a hell of a thing to be thinking about here in this damn swamp in the darkness. He didn't know what brought it on. He'd kept those memories pushed into the back of his head for a long time. Why were they resurfacing now?

He checked his watch.

"Goddammit, Drake, where the hell are you?"

As if in answer, something out in the Snakebit let out a shrill, chilling cry.

## -11-

Teague noticed that nobody was talking about what they'd seen fly from the tree and that was just fine with him. The mist, the distance, it could all play tricks with what you thought you saw. That's what he kept telling himself because he had to. He couldn't dwell on any of that because if he did, he would have marched them out of the swamp in a minute.

Denial, that's what it was.

A primary coping mechanism of humankind. If something was too devastating, too traumatic for the human mind, it was simply easier to pretend it hadn't happened in the first place. Hence, if you convinced yourself that there was no boogeyman in the closet (contrary to what you *knew* to be true), then he couldn't slip out and wrap his flaking green hands around your throat. *I do not believe in spooks, so they cannot get me. Cancer gets other people, so I have nothing to worry about.* Good old denial, a tool of self-preservation.

When Teague was nine-years-old, his mother had left him alone with his baby brother, Randy. *Don't worry,* she told him. *I'm just running to the store. I'll be back in twenty minutes. He's sleeping. He'll never even wake up. There's nothing to worry about.* But as she left, Teague *was* worried, worried as he'd never been in his short life.

He couldn't sit still.

He couldn't watch TV.

He couldn't look through his collection of football cards.

He could only listen for Randy.

There was not a peep from him for fifteen minutes and Mom would be home soon, so there really was nothing to worry about. But he was scared down deep, disturbed at his core, and nothing he told himself would change it, so he tiptoed upstairs to look in on Randy and, Christ, Mom was right: he never would wake up. His face was blue, blackening around the eyes and mouth. Teague had screamed and ran outside, shouting at the top of his lungs that his brother was dead, he had choked or suffocated, he was dead, dead, *he was fucking dead!* Maybe he hadn't used the F-word, but he'd wanted to. His aunt from across the street was the first on the scene and then the ambulance came. Mom arrived about that time, never knowing that her little trip to the store to grab some sirloin for her husband's dinner was an event that would change her life forever in the worst possible way.

Within a week, it was all over with—the funeral, the grieving, everything. Even Randy's room was cleaned out as if he had never existed. The death of Baby Randy was never, ever discussed. The child was not mentioned again.

And when Teague asked his aunt about that months later, she said, "That's how people cope. That's how they keep from losing their minds. Denial ain't just a river, son."

And that's what Teague was seeing now. They did not talk about the monstrous thing that had flown from the tree; hence, it did not exist and could do them no harm.

"How far we going this time?" Marco asked.

"Mac wants us moving. He wants us in deeper to set up a listening post, see if we can hear the shitheads."

"That shows you how he ain't thinking clearly," Labonski said. "We're talking Pegg here. He was a Marine Raider. This is exactly the sort of terrain he was trained to operate in."

"I don't give a shit what he was. He's still a man."

There was grumbling and groaning over that. The men were scared and he knew it. What happened before had unhinged them. They weren't afraid of running into Drake or Carnie, just Pegg. He was a dangerous guy that had been trained to kill.

Using their flashlights, they probed deeper into the Snakebit, walking single-file along bridges of land that cut through misting pockets of swamp and steaming open water, moving through clumped vegetation and towering stands of sawgrass that slit their hands and arms open. They fought through mud holes that sucked them in up to their thighs and chopped through unpleasantly thick stands of buttonbush. Wiles saw a big alligator in a black pool nosing through the reeds and nearly opened up on it and Corbett broke through feathery sphagnum moss and sank up to his hips in a bog.

It was hard going.

The men were picking at each other as they burned leeches from their legs, scratched at chigger bites, and were beset by swarms of mosquitoes.

Teague was desperately searching for some open high ground they could situate themselves on. Anywhere that was dry.

"How long is this going to go on for?" Labonski wanted to know. "I got ticks all over me."

"It's goddamned dangerous out here at night," Corbett said.

"Quit your bellyaching," Teague told them, even though he sympathized completely. "This is what Mac wants, so we have to do it."

"Bullshit."

"We're not paid for this kind of shit."

"What I don't get," Marco said, "is that we should have linked up with Millhaus and his boys by now. Where the hell are they?"

Teague sighed. "I don't know."

"Lost. Or the gators got them," Wiles said.

"Or snakes," Suterman added.

"Anything could have happened."

"You boys need to quit talking," Teague finally said. "If our shitheads are out there, they can hear us a mile away."

He led on, his flashlight beam peeling back the mist until finally he saw it, just ahead, what he'd been looking for: a great circular mound that rose up from the swamp. It was open land with a series of forested hills just behind it. It would be perfect. Now it was only a matter of reaching it.

"C'mon," he told them. "That's it."

It seemed like a terribly long walk. It was as if the trees were pulling away from them rather than getting closer. He saw the moon drifting above and it looked much larger than any moon he had ever seen before, a sinister orb that watched them and mocked their progress. He caught a glimpse of something with bright yellow eyes out in the swamp, but he did not mention the fact.

The ground was uneven, filled with dark pools and muddy draws, but at least it was away from open water and gators, no sawgrass or towering reed banks. Halfway there, they paused, up to their knees in the muck.

"Hell is that?" Marco asked.

They all saw it: several bouncing globes of green-yellow light flickering over the water in the distance. They seemed to be hovering there. Now that the men had stopped, the lights had stopped.

"Swamp gas," Teague said, not sure if he believed it or not. "Will-o'-the-wisp."

"Corpse candles. That's what my ma called it," Corbett said.

Whatever it was and regardless of what they called it, it was eerie and unnatural. It did not look like gas at all, but eyes, glowing eyes that were watching them, following them. Teague could feel the fear coming off the other men. He could feel it in himself, too, crawling under his skin. Then one by one, the lights went out.

"I'm never coming out here again. Swear to God," Marco said.

It might have even been funny under any other circumstance, but no one was laughing. Their mouths were sealed tight with dread. It was almost as if the Snakebit had them exactly where it wanted them, tucked away in this awful place they would never escape from. It was closing in on them, shutting them away from the real world.

Finally, they reached the mound and sat down. The shadows seemed to be crawling around them. It was good to be out of the muck and dripping undergrowth. They were all wet and miserable.

"Be nice if we could light a fire," Marco said.

But Teague told them that wasn't possible. "The shitheads would see it and know exactly where not to go."

Labonski shook his head. "Maybe you're wrong on that, Sarge. Maybe they're lost out here and it might draw them in, make them give themselves up."

"Might be a good idea," Suterman said.

"No," Teague told them. "Absolutely not. Mac would have a shit fit if we did something like that. Do I need to tell you guys how he gets when his orders aren't followed?"

"Probably nothing dry enough to burn anyway," Marco said.

Wiles grabbed Teague by the arm. "Listen. You hear that?"

They went silent and for a moment all they could hear were the night sounds of the swamp, the animals and bugs, a slight breeze whooshing through the high branches of the piney woods above them. Then they heard a cracking sound in the distance like a branch had been broken. Then another from a different direction. And a third from yet another direction. The sounds were irregular, but they all sounded very much like sticks breaking the way they would if they were stepped upon.

"Could be them," Corbett said in a weak voice. "Could be Millhaus and his boys."

Marco stood up. "I don't see any lights. If it was Millhaus and his boys, they'd have flashlights. They'd be using them."

"And why would the sounds be coming from different directions?"

Nobody wanted to field that one. Teague's throat had gone so dry again he could not speak. He wanted to tell them that sound carries funny out in the swamp, but he just didn't have the heart.

The sounds continued. Sharp and cracking, then disappearing completely, only to start up again a few minutes later. Teague noticed what they were all noticing—that the noises were getting closer each time, as if whoever was out there was slowly moving in at them from three directions.

Then the sounds stopped. They waited five minutes, then ten, and there was still nothing. Teague was staring up at the moon hanging above the pine trees, thinking about how large it was and how cold it made him feel inside. The sight of it frightened him and he had no idea why, only that he kept thinking of all the abominations it had shone down upon through the ages, all the horrors and grotesque night things. It made him feel helpless and insignificant as if it wasn't just a moon but the eye of some ancient cosmic horror. The terror it inspired in him was not just psychological, but physical, making his stomach roll over as if he had just swallowed a handful of cold, wriggling maggots.

After a few minutes, when he was thinking straight again,  he said, "Get on the radio. See if you can raise Mac."

Corbett tried again and again. "I'm not getting a thing."

"You probably need higher ground," Labonski suggested.

Teague nodded. "Could be. Take it up on the high ground by the trees. Try it up there."

Corbett hesitated.

"Oh, for chrissake, I'll go with you," Suterman said.

"Be careful," Marco warned them. "Watch where you're stepping."

They started off and Corbett didn't seem very happy about it. Teague didn't blame him, but, hell, they had a job to do. Sitting around like this, letting their imaginations run wild because of cracking sticks just wouldn't do. He watched them leave the mound, climbing up the slope above very slowly and carefully. There was a moment of unease as they disappeared behind a cluster of bushes, then he saw them again, two dark shapes moving up toward the trees. Their flashlight beams bounced around and he thought he heard Corbett grumbling.

Teague was going to call out to them to hurry it along, but his voice dried up in his throat. A weird, unearthly shrieking rose up out in the Snakebit, a screeching and terrible sound that increased in volume before breaking apart and echoing around them like the guttural laughter of hyenas.

"Oh, Jesus, what the hell is that?" Wiles asked.

But Teague couldn't answer because it was like nothing he'd ever heard before. It was doglike in a way, but squealing like that of a wild boar. And even that wasn't quite it. In the back of his mind, a voice told him that if a ghost had a voice, it would sound like that.

And then up near the trees, he heard Suterman scream the way a man had no right to scream. "I SAW IT!" he cried. "IT'S RIGHT THERE! OH CHRIST IT'S RIGHT THERE—"

And then there was the sound of gunfire. Not one or two shots, but the sound of a .38 being emptied and then the *click-click-click* of empty chambers.

Then they were all charging through the darkness to their aid, stumbling and tripping, finding roots and crevices. And there was movement all around them, shapes circling them in the night, leaping around them and over them, disappearing when flashlight beams sought them out. A peal of that terrible laughter. A feral snarling. Marco and the others cried out, shouting and grunting, opening fire in all directions and then whatever had been moving around them was gone as if it had never been there in the first place.

Teague reached the top and he saw Suterman standing there like a post, his eyes huge in the flashlight beam, his mouth hanging open. He was drenched in blood, looking as if he'd been dipped in red ink. It glistened on him and dripped from the empty .38 in his hand. The men gasped and made whining sounds in their throats. The blood was shining in the yellow grass, too, and there was a good reason for that: Corbett was spread in every direction as if he had literally exploded. His torso was an open trench. One of his legs was three feet away. A hand, still clutching his .38, was farther away still. And behind all this, dangling from the tree branches were his entrails, still steaming, still dripping.

<h2 style="text-align:center">-12-</h2>

Things were going to shit and Gus knew it. He didn't have a watch, but he knew they were late, very late, for the rendezvous with Pegg. Drake kept getting them lost. Starting in one direction, realizing he'd lost the trail, then backtracking until they'd picked it up again.

If Pegg wasn't there when they arrived, Drake and Swede would kill him and he didn't honestly believe that Carnie would be able to stop it.

Despite that odd and foul odor creeping up from time to time, Gus had no more mishaps. He concentrated on what he was doing and slowly gained confidence, but not enough to wander freely without thoroughly testing each foothold before stepping. He wasn't sure whether it was his imagination or not, but the night seemed to be getting colder. And it wasn't a gradual thing: moments before he was bathed in sweat, the damp chill pretty much forgotten, but now he was shivering. His fingers actually felt numb.

But that was crazy.

It was the middle of July.

His temples were beginning to throb and he was quite sure he was coming down with something.

Maybe the cold air meant they were nearing the sea. That was possible.

"Hold it!" Drake called out, fanning his arms out. Swede stopped dead and Gus rammed right into him. It was like rear-ending a Peterbuilt. He went down on his ass, his head pounding uncontrollably now.

"Listen," Swede said. "Up ahead...something..."

The knotted growth before them was ghostly, wrapped in tendrils of fog. Only black branches jutted out. They looked eerily like the broomstick arms of skeletons.

"What—" Gus began.

"Shut your hole!" Drake snapped, but in a whisper as if he was afraid he might be heard.

Gus was still down and he stayed that way. He listened, very aware of the blood pulsing in his ears, the breath in his lungs. He couldn't see anything, just the mist and the darkness…but he could hear something. Brush crackling, branches snapping, like something was moving out there. Something big.

He looked at the vague forms of his companions. Looking for strength and surely for leadership, but getting neither. They were silent, waiting. If he hadn't known better, he would've sworn they were scared.

Licking his dry lips, he listened with them. It was still very cold, yet he was sweating. Tiny rivers of perspiration ran down his brow. And out there in that dark unknown something was moving. But moving didn't do this justice. It was the huge, angry sound of something immense crashing through the woods. And with it came that horrible smell again. Festering, rotten. The air turned into a noxious, gaseous envelope of vile decay.

Gus wished he were back in his cell. Not out here in this evil desolation with that tomblike odor and something … *evil* circling them as if it were trying to find them like a blind man clawing in darkness. Any minute now, he knew, it would find them.

The smell grew positively poisonous.

Gus had to steel himself so he didn't retch.

It was out there, yes, closer, closer. Huge, gigantic, dreadful, dragging its immense rotting hide through the night. Gus felt the need to scream, to vent. Then a low, bestial growling rose up all around them and shattered into a dozen separate shrill screechings before fading altogether. Gus was hugging himself, his body shaking violently. The air was so incredibly cold he could see his breath, but the cold, the real cold, was deep inside like his bones had gone to ice.

The growling started again, a deep, guttural sound that, became a high, ear-piercing scream. But not just one, but dozens it seemed. A hundred lost souls screaming out their despair.

Then everything went very quiet.

The smell lessened and vanished. The air suddenly didn't feel so cold.

A slight breeze began to blow. It was just night again. Ordinary night. The crickets started chirping. Owls hooted. The night world had held its breath and now it let it out.

Carnie pulled him to his feet and Gus could feel the man was drenched in cold sweat. He was shivering violently. Gus's flesh was creeping on his bones and his head felt oddly heavy. Filled, perhaps, with things it simply could not deal with.

"What the fuck was that?" Swede demanded.

"An animal, maybe ... I don't know," Drake said in an empty voice.

"Let's get the hell out of here," Gus suggested.

And, for once, they agreed with him.

## -13-

In the thick of the marshes, the dogs lost the scent.

Maybe they didn't have it in the first place. Lofquist cajoled them, threatened them, petted them, but none of it did any good. They stopped dead, then chased their own tails, started barking at shadows and snarling and snapping at one another. He tried to be patient with them. God knew he loved those damn bloodhounds more than anything on this earth, but now they were embarrassing him and he didn't like it.

"Your mutts are fucking worthless," McClaren told him. "Bunch of poodles. Jesus H. Christ."

"Dammit, they're the best. I bred 'em and raised 'em myself. I never seen 'em act like this."

"Yeah, well, maybe you're too old for this game."

"Fuck you, Mac. You don't know what you're talking about."

*Oh boy, here we go,* Underwood thought. *Here's where the chain of command goes belly-up.*

Mac said, "Get them on the trail of my shitheads or I'll fucking shoot them. Swear to God I will."

"You better watch it with that."

The dogs, sensing the hostility being directed at their master, stalked slowly in Mac's direction, hackles raised, teeth bared.

"You try something like that," Lofquist said, "and I won't be able to pull them off you."

Mac backed down. "All right. Just get 'em moving."

Lofquist shouted a few commands and the dogs began to cast for scent again. Meanwhile, Mac got on his walkie-talkie and tried contacting the other search parties. He couldn't raise either of them and they were too far away from the prison now to report in.

"Goddamn warden must be having kittens about now," Underwood said.

"Her own fault. We shouldn't have tried any of this before first light," Peters pointed out.

"Stop jabbering," Mac warned them.

Then he went over to Keye and Charney and gave them a ration of shit for no apparent reason.

Underwood waited there with his riot gun. Peters, at his side, did the same thing.

This was going to be a bust and he knew it. They were going to go in circles all damned night. By first light, they'd be no closer to getting Pegg and the others. For all they knew, the escapees were already off the island. Underwood hoped it was true. Sooner they were off Despair the sooner they could wash their hands of them.

It was going to be a long night.

The dogs weren't grabbing any scent at all. Lofquist was getting frustrated and McClaren was barely holding himself together as he watched his future going down the toilet.

The hounds started howling.

They cowered around Lofquist's legs as if they were scared of something. He tried to shake them off. He pushed them, he kicked at them, he shouted at them, but there was absolutely no reasoning with them. They were large, sleek, powerful animals, but right then they were meek as kittens. They acted like they'd just picked up the scent of a Bengal tiger.

"Hell's wrong with 'em now?" McClaren wanted to know.

"Can't figure it," Lofquist said. "Just can't figure the way they're acting."

It was then that the smell came back, stronger than ever. The dogs whimpered and the men swore, pinching their noses shut. It wasn't just the smell of death, but the stink of a hundred graves opening simultaneously. A tomb odor that was thick and putrescent and just plain sickening.

Then, like before, it was just gone.

"Christ," Peters said. "What the hell was that?"

"It's the swamp. That's all it is," McClaren said. "Place is full of rotting, dead things. Quit going on about it."

Underwood said nothing. He could sense the uneasiness and anxiety that had gripped Mac. There was no denying it. He could stomp around and swear and pump himself up, but inside he was afraid.

"Smelled like a graveyard," Peters said.

"Quit imagining shit," McClaren told him without much conviction.

"Ain't nothing natural smells like that," Lofquist said. "I know it and my dogs know it. Whatever it is, we're getting close now. Real close."

No one bothered arguing with him. Least of all Underwood who knew he was right. Lofquist was a local and an old hand at tracking fugitives. He knew his business and he knew the kind of things that happened in the Snakebit sometimes. Maybe he wasn't mentioning any of it, but he was thinking it, Underwood knew. Thinking about it and it was scaring the shit out of him even if he didn't say so.

The dogs picked up something and off everyone went on the merry chase again.

"What could smell like that?" Peters asked about ten minutes later as they navigated roots and black pools of mud, well out of earshot of McClaren.

Underwood shrugged. "Don't know, son. But I figure whatever it is, we're right on the cusp of it. We're standing in the doorway of its world and it's looking right at us."

## -14-

As the night progressed, Warden Keafer found herself becoming more and more angry, frustrated, and just plain hopeless. Her blood was beginning to boil and its source was the following: five escaped prisoners, a dead guard, and a certain Lieutenant of the Guard, graveyard shift, named Warren S. McClaren. A man she had placed great trust in and who she had actually promoted from sergeant to lieutenant.

And a man who led the search teams after the escapees and also a man she had not heard from in nearly two hours now.

*You know damn well what it means,* she told herself, *and the sort of horrific mess it entails.*

Oh, she knew, all right.

And she shouldn't have been surprised.

McClaren was good at his job, yes, but he was also stubborn, arrogant, and overly confident, thinking his way must be the right way every time. He was well-known for being pig-headed, blunt, and completely lacking in skills of diplomacy. But despite these things (and perhaps because of them), he got things done. He motivated his men. He kept the prisoners in line. And he fastidiously played by the rules.

When they discussed options following the escape, the warden's plan was simple and, she thought, effective: men patrolling the fields and woods, the water's edge, and the very outer perimeter of Snakebit Swamp. But under no circumstances did she want any of her people entering the swamp by night.

That was imperative.

"Ma'am," McClaren said, "we've got a guard that's been murdered in cold blood. We have to take whatever action is necessary to run those shitheads to ground."

"Which will not include entering the Snakebit by night," she impressed upon him. "It's too dangerous. Stackhouse has lost too many prisoners out there and far too many officers searching for them. And that will not happen on my watch." Here she paused. "Do I make myself clear?"

"Yes, ma'am. But keep in mind Danny Clayton. If it gets out that we didn't do everything we could to apprehend his killer … well, it's not going to reflect very favorably on us and I think you know that. The newspapers will be juggling our heads."

She nodded. "And in the morning, we'll have people from the sheriff's office, the state police, and the national guard at our disposal. Along with logistical support, reinforcements, and dog teams to do the job properly. I'm not going to have my men dying out in those swamps on some half-ass turkey shoot."

"Yes, ma'am."

But she'd seen the glint in his eyes, the smirk on his mouth. And, God, how many times had she seen that through the years until it left her cold right to her roots? Translated, it meant, *sure, sure, but you're a woman and what could you possibly know about such things?* And looking back now, she was certain that McClaren never had any intention of following her orders. He, of course, knew better. He had taken the death of one of his guards as a personal affront. There was no way he could be expected to act professionally. He was a bully at heart and another bully had kicked sand in his face. His over-inflated male ego demanded that he get even at all costs.

*And he's bucking for captain, too,* she thought. *Well, that's one thing he'll never get. Not after this.*

If McClaren sent his men into the Snakebit, it was going to be an unimaginable mess. The need for damage control would be high and she didn't even know where to begin. *They'll say you lost control of your people. That you're a woman in a man's job.* For the past two hours, she'd been fielding calls from the county sheriff, the state police, and the BOP. From the undercurrent of the former, she knew they thought exactly that and from the latter, that the future of Louisiana's first female warden was seriously in doubt.

On her desk was the very file that Underwood had alluded to. It was kept in the safe, passed from warden to warden, but was never, ever available to anyone else. Lighting a cigarette, she paged through it, narrowing her eyes at the list of convicts that had disappeared in the depths of the Snakebit and wincing at the list of correctional officers and sheriff's deputies that had been lost trying to find them. She looked through photographs and mug shots, scanned accounts given by those who had survived the horrors of the swamp, those things they had claimed to have seen.

She closed the file, shaking her head and exhaling a cloud of smoke. "Nonsense. It has to be all nonsense," she said under her breath. "Tall tales. Folklore. Spook stories."

When she had been appointed the state's first female warden, bypassing many men much better qualified, she suspected she was being used in some game of partisan manipulation. And that, unfortunately, proved to be true. Franklin Blowden, the commissioner of the BOP, had used every bit of political leverage he had and called in every possible favor, making promises and threats, using out-and-out coercion, everything at his disposal to put her through. The members of the board of directors had been staunchly against the idea of a woman running a mens' correctional institute. But Blowden broke them down one by one. And it wasn't because he was a defender of women's equality, but because of his long-standing feud with Raul Murkinson of the DOJ, who had long been a thorn in his side. Murkinson came from old Southern money, very traditional and very conservative. The very idea of a female warden was an insult to him personally and all that he stood for. Women made pies and hosted teas and got pregnant, but they sure as hell did not run prisons.

But Blowden pulled it off, giving his enemy not only a slap in the face, but a kick in the ass that he would never recover from.

After Keafer was appointed, Blowden told her, "I stuck my neck out for you, Margaret. I'm right up against the wall on this one. It won't be enough for you to be just a good warden, you'll need to be ten times the warden any man has ever been. You need to become a legend. You need to be so good that you can wipe your ass with the records of your predecessors."

In other words, if she didn't pull it off, Louisiana wouldn't see another female warden for fifty years.

And now this.

Now this.

There was a knock at the door just as she was wondering what her head might look like on a silver platter. It was Eagleton, the deputy warden. He looked even more dour than usual.

"Ma'am," he said. "We finally reached Danny Clayton's mother. She's on line two."

Warden Keafer swallowed. "Put her through."

This was where a bad situation became positively ugly.

## -15-

The entire thing was a bust and Pegg knew it.

There was no way in hell they could make the boat now. He could have, but that would have meant leaving the kid behind and he just couldn't do that. This had been the one. Five years to set up and now it was gone. The only chance he'd ever had.

*You could hide out in the Snakebit for weeks or months, wait for an opportunity to cross.*

But without knowing what had happened to the kid, he knew it wouldn't happen.

He had no choice now.

He had to go back.

He had to find Drake and the others if the bulls hadn't already caught them, which, of course, was a very strong possibility. Either way, he was going to have words with Drake. Whether that was out here or back behind bars, he was going to get that sonofabitch and the BOP would see to it that he had plenty of time in which to do it.

But what he didn't know and what he was vaguely beginning to guess in the back of his mind was that going back inside would be the least of his problems.

## -16-

"We should have hooked up with Pegg an hour ago," Carnie said. "He's going to hang someone's ass out to dry and it won't be mine."

"Shut the hell up," Drake told him. "If he had been where he said he was going to be, none of this would have happened."

"Oh, it's his fault?"

"Maybe you took us on a wrong turn back there," Swede suggested.

"The fuck I did."

Gus kept his mouth shut while they bickered back and forth. Though he was miserable in this damn swamp and in a very dangerous position, he was kind of enjoying the growing animosity between Swede and Drake. They were nearly constantly picking at each other and that made him smile inside.

"Everything was timed out," Swede said. "You know that. Pegg said if we fucked up, if we were so much as a half an hour late, it would make a mess of things. We'd miss our pick-up and that would be the end of things."

"Quit squawking," Drake told him, but the tension under his words was strung tight.

"Well, that's that," Carnie said. He pulled a cigarette from the pocket of his stripes and lit it up, seeing no reason not to now. "Only a matter of time until those dogs track us down."

Swede grunted. "Pegg probably grabbed that boat and is miles away by now."

"You think so?" Drake said, picking what teeth he had with a sharp little stick. "You really think he'd leave his boy behind? His punk bitch?"

"I ain't anybody's punk bitch!" Gus snapped.

That made Drake laugh. "Ain't what I hear. Word has it you're sucking his dick and spreading your cheeks for him. You like that stuff." He kept laughing his dry, degenerate laugh that sounded like a man choking to death. "Go ahead, kid. Get pissed-off. Get good and mad. Then you can come over here and sort me out. Pegg ain't here to protect you and there ain't no hogs to pull me off you."

Gus felt suddenly sick to his stomach. He didn't know if it was what Drake was saying or the heat and exhaustion, the stink of brackish water and mud and rotting vegetation or all of it. He slapped at skeeters on his neck, leaving blood splotches on his throat, and pulled ticks from his arms. As the nausea faded, it was replaced by anger, by rage. He had all he could do not to launch himself right at Drake and thumb the eyes from his head. Drake would kill him, but he found that he didn't care.

"If Pegg's not putting it to you, he's missing a treat," Drake said, still laughing with that guttural sound low in his throat. "Maybe me and Swede will break you in right now."

"Knock it off," Carnie said. "We ain't got time for that shit. We gotta find that trail and get to Pegg. We can't just sit here."

"And who put you in charge?"

Carnie cleared his throat and spit into the grass. "I put me in charge because you've fucked this whole thing up right from the beginning."

Drake was on his feet with a shank in his hand, the same one he'd killed the guard with.

"You better sit down," Carnie warned him. "If I gotta get up and sort you out, I won't stop until you're bleeding out. I give you five seconds, you stupid fucking mutt."

"You think you can handle me *and* Swede?"

Swede shook his head. "Not me. Fuck that. I just want to get out of here."

Now it was up to Drake. Gus watched him carefully in the moonlight. Drake was dangerous and he knew it, but like most bullies he was a coward at heart. He liked to go after the weak and defenseless. The ones that didn't fight back. He did his best work when your back was turned, just like he'd done with Danny Clayton. But he didn't have the stomach for face to face action and particularly with Carnie, who was a real expert with a blade in his hand.

He lowered himself down slowly. He was not beaten and Gus knew it; just biding his time was all, homicide brewing in his heart.

"Okay, boss man, okay. What's our plan?"

Carnie thought it over carefully. "I don't think we've got time to backtrack. My guess is that we're in the right general area. Pegg said there was a stream running past where he'd be waiting. There's a stream right over there. Let's get to it, follow it, hope he hears us coming."

"Gotta be hundreds of streams out here," Swede said.

"Sure, but like I said, I don't think we're too far away from where we're supposed to be. It's worth a shot."

Swede grumbled.

Drake swore.

But when Carnie got up and started moving, they followed him right to the stream, a creek that was wide and dark and rushing in the light of the moon. Thick underbrush overhung it except where it was worn away by animal trails and rock outcroppings.

The moonlight was very bright, making the creek look like a winding silver ribbon. The trees and bushes seemed to glow. The mist coming from the swamps and sinkholes looked practically luminous.

"What's that smell?" Gus asked.

They ignored him. There was no way they couldn't have smelled it. It was a gagging, enormous stink that was sweet, musky, and utterly repellent. For Gus, it was like he'd thrust his head into the bowels of a decaying beehive. It smelled like that, only worse. And there was something under it, something dark and vile that he didn't like.

It didn't seem to bother Swede, though.

He was telling one of his prison stories as the opaque swamp fog rolled in and Drake stood there, biding his time, considering his options as men like him did. Gus wished yet again he was still in his cell—something that amazed even him—instead of out here in the damn Snakebit where the insects outnumbered men a hundred-million to one at the very least. There were fleas nipping at his neck and chiggers biting at his arms.

A skink ran across his shoe and he spit at it.

The smell vanished ... and then it came right back, only stronger.

He was about to comment on it when he felt a huge surge of hot air rush over him and something hit him, knocking him over into the knife grass, his face submerging in the miasmic waters of the creek. But as he went down he saw—thought he saw—something hit Carney. It seemed to leap out of the fog. He pulled his face out of the water and a spray of blood and meat struck him and he was down again.

Crying out, he wiped the ichor from his eyes.

But Carney was gone. Just … gone.

There was gore splattered in the grass. It was dripping down Gus's face like red tears. And at his feet, there was a muddy boot with a stump of ankle jutting from it.

"What the hell?" he heard Swede say.

"RUN!" Drake cried out. "FOR CHRIST'S SAKE, RUN!"

He saw one of Carney's arms floating down the steaming creek. And then that sweet, sickening stench came again. Fantastic forms seemed to move in the fog around them.

Then they were all running into the swamp and its thick foliage, away from the open hunting grounds of the creek.

## -17-

It was miserable country, black and dirty and stinking, a primeval hellhole and even that didn't cover it. Mac followed close behind Lofquist and the dogs, crusted with mud and swollen with bug bites, wet right up to the hips from fording streams and stagnant, green-scummed ponds. The absolutely amazing (and disheartening thing) was that he'd worked on Despair Island for years now and never once in that time had he been into the Snakebit. It was something he viewed from afar or heard tall tales about, something that he kept at arm's length, but never gave much thought to.

And now, here he was, in the thick of it, hunting his shitheads and it was worse than anything he could have imagined.

The Snakebit was either eerie and deadly silent or it was loud with shrieking night birds, chittering and lowing noises, buzzing insects and droning cicadas. Even the high ground was treacherous with crevices and mud holes that would suck you in up to your knees, low-hanging tree branches that would slap you in the face, stinging nettles and ferns crawling with spiders. It was a primordial place of steaming bogs and black marshes, razor grass and stands of reeds that towered over your head. It was easy to get turned around, hopping rotting logs and circling around deadfalls, ducking under pine and tupelo branches, clawing through hanging moss and dangling parasitic vines. Everything was wet and slimy to the touch. They forded ponds and open swamp, up to their hips in the muck, carrying the damn dogs so they didn't drown.

And all the while, the heat broiled you inside your own skin, your uniform plastered with sweat to your body, your boots filled with mud and rank water, leeches on your legs and down the small of your back.

The men were ornery, snapping at each other and swearing at the dogs. But what it all came down to, Mac knew, was that they blamed him.

*The warden told you not to go out here at night*, he taunted himself. *But you knew better. She was just a woman and you weren't about to listen to her and now where the hell are you?*

They were pushing through heavy undergrowth now and, God, why hadn't they brought machetes? The dogs were really getting excited. They had something and they weren't going to stop until they ran it to ground. Lofquist seemed to have very little control over them—it was almost as if they had gone feral, answering some call of the wild, becoming increasingly ferocious. They dragged him behind them like a rag doll and it took everything Mac had to keep up.

The hounds moved up a series of low, grassy hills, splashing through the muddy water in-between, moving, moving, scenting, barking and howling. Mac tripped over a root and went down in the slop. Underwood and Peters pulled him up and he fought free of them and he knew, God yes, that if he came upon his shitheads right now he would have killed every last one of them.

And then the dogs stopped, tangled up in their leads, whining and snapping at one another. Flashlight beams found tall grass glistening with dew. But then with a sinking feeling in his guts, Mac knew it wasn't dew at all; it was too red, far too red.

"Oh, Jesus," Charney said, turning away with Keye.

Their lights had picked out something like a post or a jutting sapling and speared atop it was a human head. The face was cream-white, splattered with blood that looked black. One eye was swollen closed, the other wide and glazed with what might have been terror, the mouth sprung in a silent scream.

There was no doubt who it was.

"Corbett," Underwood said. "That's Corbett's head."

And Mac sank to his knees, trying not to throw his guts out, trying to understand this and put it into some kind of perspective. This was a nightmare scenario and his mind whirled inside his head as fever sweat dripped from his jawline.

He only knew one thing for sure: Corbett's head had not been taken off cleanly the way an axe might do it. No, there was a confetti of raw meat and ligament hanging from the neck stump, a section of vertebrae. Corbett's head hadn't been chopped off, it had been ripped from his body.

## -18-

For a moment there, Pegg thought he'd finally get his hands on Drake. He heard his boys out in the Snakebit, shouting and yelling, stumbling about and crashing through the underbrush like they were trying to alert every goddamn hog on the island as to their location.

He even saw them by moonlight, charging into the heavy growth. What bothered him about that was that there were only three shapes, but he was certain that one of them was Gus. The problem was, he was separated from them by a series of wide ponds that he would have had to swim across to reach them. He had no choice but to circle far around the open water and by that time, they'd be long gone.

Even now, their sounds were fading into the distance.

*Dammit. Dammit all to hell.*

Somehow, someway, they'd lost a man, and Pegg grew angry because in his way of thinking, Drake was to blame. That stupid sonofabitch couldn't do anything right.

But he knew he couldn't distract himself with that. He had to get to them first. He circled around the ponds, edging as close as he could, ducking under primrose and bog willow, pushing through stands of dogwood and heavy brush. It was bottomland hardwood forest, the ground soft and potholed, his feet slipping on moist clay. He was making too much noise and he knew it, but he didn't have time to be quiet. He had to catch up with them. He had to set things right ... or as right as they could be in this mess.

Every now and again, he paused, listening. He could still hear them, but they were getting farther away with every passing second.

He was making good time, but he honestly didn't think it would be enough. Then he tripped on a root, tried to catch himself, and tripped on another. He went down, rolling through the undergrowth into a dry hollow filled with some kind of thorny brush like brambles. The thorns tore at his face, slit open his outstretched arms, and snagged his clothing. He was snarled in them, swearing and fighting himself free and making all manner of noise.

When he finally got free, he was bruised and cut, face painted with blood, his shirt ripped open in five or six places. His forearms looked like they'd been slashed with a razor.

On higher ground, he lay there, panting, dripping with sweat. It had been a long time since he'd done any night patrol and it was no longer second nature to him. Too many years in a cell had blunted his edge, dulled his instincts. He was making too much noise, fumbling and awkward and out of his element.

*If Mac and his hogs are out there, you've just announced your position.*

And that worried him more than just about anything else: that he wouldn't reach the others in time. If Drake thought he had abandoned him, the kid would pay for it. Pegg was sure of it. Drake was just looking for a reason to stick a shank in him.

As exhausted as he was, as beaten up, cut and bloodied, he began to crawl faster and faster until he finally got to his feet and started to really move, parting the awful, cloying mists of the swamps and slowly, slowly closing in on his target.

He would get to them or die trying.

## -19-

The situation was not only bleak, it was a nightmare. Corbett was dead. The radio was gone. Teague's men were terrified. There was no discipline left. Now and again, they opened up with their rifles and revolvers at shadows or bushes, out of their minds with fear. They were hunched together like frightened schoolboys and there wasn't a damn thing Teague could tell them to make them act like men again.

"We're lost," Marco said. "And that thing's going to pick us off one by one."

"But what is it?" Wiles wanted to know, his voice high and squeaky like that of a boy. "What did that to Corbett?"

"A monster," Labonski said.

All eyes, of course, were on Suterman, but he was unaware of the fact. He had not spoken since it happened and Teague had a feeling he never would again, not without a long stay in a hospital.

"All right, can the monster talk," Teague told them. "Our job now is to get the hell out of here. It's important that we think about only that."

Marco chuckled with more than a little sarcasm. "And how do we do that? We're lost. We're fucking lost."

"We'll backtrack. That's all we can do."

That radio had been their lifeline, he knew, and they were in a real fix without it. They had searched high and low for it and it was just gone. But at night with all the undergrowth it would have been easy to miss. He wasn't going to start thinking that what had gotten Corbett had purposely taken the radio to cut them off. Because if that was true, if it was that smart, they were done.

He allowed no more time for discussion; he simply couldn't afford it. He was in charge. He had gotten them out here and he was going to get them out again.

The Snakebit by night was eerie and unsettling. Plumes of mist rose from the marshes, gathering in ghostly patches that drifted around like phantoms. In the distance, it appeared luminous and flickering. Along the edges of the swamp was a sea of thick, clustering sawgrass that slit open hands and faces with tiny papercuts. It rose up in shivering stalks eight and nine feet in height. They pushed through it, feeling it rustling against them, their faces breaking through dewy spiderwebs. Alien-looking cypresses grew from the water with their attendant root systems, or *knees,* breaking the surface.

Teague parted the grasses with the barrel of his .30-06, studying the trees and the encroaching, steaming bogs. Islands of moss and mats of reeds floated on their surface, along with bladderwort and arrowhead.

As he walked, every sense heightened, each foot placed carefully, he wrinkled his nose at the noxious smells rising from the water. It was a pungent, subterranean sort of stink, a sewer-smell and a death-smell, the stench of miasmic organic rot.

The stifling heat and humidity were sapping the strength from him, swarms of bloodsucking insects circling his head. This was a place of death and decay, perhaps something beyond those things.

As sweat rolled down his face and leeches inched up his legs, he began to believe there was something primeval, prehistoric even, about Snakebit Swamp. It was a misting, stinking mire straight out of the Cretaceous. Gigantic spreading ferns and thick, lush vegetation, nets of moss and strangling green vines hanging from the trees. Even the gators they'd seen seemed unnaturally large.

Had a dinosaur raised its slime-dripping snout from the waterlogged reeds, he somehow would not have been surprised.

Slapping at mosquitoes, eyes bugging from his head, he forced himself to calm down. No easy thing in that wet, green hell.

*You can't come apart now,* he cautioned himself. *You're the only thing holding these boys together. Without you leading them, they'd panic and scatter to the four winds.*

Yes, he had to keep his head above water. Even if he was only holding himself together with spit and lies, he couldn't let them know it.

And he definitely couldn't let them see the abject terror threading through him or know that he thought this place was evil, from mud to frond to tree, just black and seething with it. His imagination kept telling him that they'd never escape. That days from now, they'd still be here, wandering in circles, stricken mad…or that weeks from now, their white bones would be sunk in the black, bubbling mud.

"There's things out there," Wiles said. "I can hear 'em."

They all could, of course. Squealing noises, piping and squawking sounds. The swamp was alive and busy. Things splashed through the water and crept through the brush. The reeds shook from time to time even though there was no discernable breeze and the stands of sawgrass rustled as if something was shaking them.

Marco suddenly seized Teague's arm, making him jump.

"I swear I saw something move out there," he whispered.

Teague was watching carefully by then.

Flashlight beams were spoking in every which direction—trying to pierce the pockets of mist that clung to the marshes, shining off the swaying reeds and up into the trees. One of them was pointing straight up into the sky.

Something splashed out in the fog.

There was a flapping sound like sails filling with air.

Several tree branches broke free of a gnarled cypress and crashed into the water.

And then, from what seemed three or four different locations in the night world, there came a braying, fragmented cry that rose to a high-pitched shrilling before becoming the evil laughter of a hyena before fading away entirely. Everyone knew that sound because they'd heard it right before Corbett was killed.

"It's coming," Wiles said, more to himself than the others.

A hot wind parted the mist, making the grass and reeds shake violently. It blew right into the faces of the men with a noisome stink like a mass grave erupting with dozens of maggoty corpses.

Teague shouted at his men to hold together, but it did little good; they were broken. Nerves had been frayed and stretched to the breaking point. Now they snapped.

Suterman clasped hands to his ears as that awful laughter once again echoed from the swamp fog. He stumbled back, knocking Wiles down, tripping and stumbling, finally screaming at the top of his lungs.

Marco and Labonski began firing into the mist, shooting at things only they could see. Rounds drilled into the water and grassy hummocks, punched holes in trees and made rotten stumps explode.

"KNOCK IT OFF!" Teague shouted. "CEASE FIRE! GODDAMMIT, CEASE FIRE!"

But it seemed to make them spend more cartridges rather than less. They kept at it until there was the clicking of empty chambers. And even then, they kept jerking triggers.

The world had gone absolutely mad.

Teague felt stunned, dazed as if he was shell-shocked. His men had suffered a collective nervous breakdown. Not that he blamed them— they were trapped in a nightmare.

The grasses and reeds were swaying, the mist churning as if it was whipped by an eggbeater. That hot stink was blowing in from every quarter. Shadows and long-armed shapes seemed to be jumping around them.

More than once now, Teague heard a flapping from above and a sort of swooshing sound. He knew it was from the sort of thing they'd seen leap from the tree earlier and the same sort of thing that had slaughtered Corbett.

Then he saw it.

While Labonski and Marco tripped over each other trying to get away, Teague caught sight of it thirty-feet out in the water on a floating island of sedge, swamp gas spiraling around it—a black shape that watched him with bright, purple-red eyes. It let out a deafening howl and its wings snapped open like wet umbrellas.

Then ... then it was flying at him, a soaring night-shape of black crêpe that seemed to glide with incredible velocity. It would have him. It would gut him, tear him open like a carcass. Then he remembered the rifle in his hands. He brought it up and shot at it. A clean miss. But it changed its trajectory and swooped over his head, its cold shadow falling over him and that graveyard stink engulfing him.

It was coming again.

This time he could not miss. He aimed, levered, and fired. He hit it. It let out a wild squawking sound that was pure rage and pain. As it soared over him again, making for the depths of the swamp, it showered him with a fine spray of black blood that ran down his face like drops of ink. It drunkenly skipped over the water, trying to climb a dead tree, and he fired at it again, this time catching it in the head. An eruption of blood and meat ejected from its skull and sprayed over the water.

*Got it! I got the sonofabitch!*

It made a pathetic mewling sound and fell backwards, flopping into the water and sinking from sight.

And then Wiles screamed.

Screamed as if he was being peeled by a very hot blade. Labonski and Marco were firing their .38s, but at what, Teague could not be sure. He was only aware that Suterman was crouched in the grass, hugging himself and whimpering like a baby. And Wiles...was just gone.

Then he heard him screaming again, but this time it came from high overhead: *"OH PLEASE! OH GOD HELP ME! SOMEBODY HELP ME—"*

His cries echoed out and out, finally disappearing in the darkness of the sky as if he was making for the stars themselves.

### -20-

They stumbled through the moonlit swamp, tripping over limbs and catching branches across the face that left red, hurting welts. The water was brown as mud and warm like some primeval soup. They fought and swore and strained. Gus found a submerged root with his ankle and pitched face-first into the muck.

Drake grasped his arm and yanked him up. "Watch where you're going, you fucking idiot," he gasped, his wide piggish face spattered with grime and beaded with sweat. Mosquitoes dotted his brow like acne, some of them swollen red with his blood. He slapped at them, catching one and smearing a stain of red across his forehead like war paint. A split second after his hand retreated, a dozen others descended to feed. "Just keep going! Keep going!"

Gus was trembling and shaking, his face slimed with Carney's anatomy. *"I saw it!"* he cried, his eyes wet. "I saw it! I saw it take Carney! I saw—"

Drake slapped him across the face and it sounded sharp as a pistol shot. "Get a hold of yourself, do you hear me? We don't have time for your little boy bullshit!"

He shoved Gus forward and Gus fell again, pulling himself up, moaning. He dragged himself through the waist-deep swamp, navigating the waterlogged tree roots, mumbling to himself about Carney, about the thing that had taken him.

He never saw what waited for him.

It looked like the hull of a submerged canoe plated with bony dorsal ridges as it moved through the brown, slopping water. It glided past Swede and zeroed in on him. Maybe it knew a straggler when it saw one, a weak link in the chain.

Drake saw the protruding reptilian eyes. When it was within four feet of Gus it roared from the water, jaws opening to reveal teeth sharp as steak knives.

Gus screamed.

"GATOR!" Swede shouted.

Gus just stood there, eyes glazed.

It was a moment of utter fear and utter clarity for him. He stood there, waiting for the monster to take him, knowing full well that neither Swede nor Drake would intervene on his behalf. And how could they? The only weapons they had were homemade knives. He could have fled, jumped out of the way, something, anything. Everything moved like molasses; he had the time. Then Drake grabbed his arm and yanked him away and the big gator, obviously not that interested in the first place, turned and slid into deep water.

"Get moving," Drake said.

"High ground ahead," Swede called back to them. "Not far."

The hot and stagnant air was suddenly thick with a flock of screeching and flapping birds, disturbed from their roosts by these invaders. They passed over the trees and shit white globs down on the men below. Drake caught a gray smear across the neck, another on his tattooed forearm. Everywhere, the shit fell, raining into the water and tangled foliage, sounding like gravel being dropped from above.

"Fucking birds!" Drake cried. "Goddamn fucking birds!"

A cypress tree came to life as hundreds of leathery bats began to squeak and chirp and stretch their wings. There were so many it seemed the tree was suddenly alive, a perpetual motion machine of claws and wings and sharp vampiric ears.

"Damn things," Drake said. "I hate fucking bats."

Gus, as dazed and confused as he was, nearly laughed. Bats. He was afraid of bats. That was sort of funny when you considered what had taken Carney.

Up ahead in the stagnant, oily water, Swede said, "Quit wasting time! We need to get out of this damn water!"

Drake followed, pushing Gus along in front of him.

What an awful place this was, Gus thought. A hideous green world of perpetual growth and stinking rot populated by clouds of biting insects, poisonous spiders, venomous snakes, and huge gators. And apparently something much, much worse.

Swede led them away from the tangled cypresses, through thick floating mats of reed, and around sucking black holes that could swallow a man alive. He kept his eyes peeled for the slow, terrible motion and telltale snouts of big gators waiting in the murky water.

He got them to dry land, to the verge of the sawgrass and its steaming, rank heat.

Drake shoved Gus up onto the bank and clawed his way out of the clotted marsh grass into the moist sand, panting and pissed-off. Lizards sprung away through the growth. The ground was soggy and spongy, but it was ground. Sweet, solid ground. And on the ground a man had a chance.

They clustered there, the three of them, waiting, wondering. Swede lit a cigarette and started burning the leeches from them. Gus had thirty of them on his legs alone. They disgusted him, but there were worse things.

Like whatever had gotten Carney.

## -21-

The tension had been building ever since they found Corbett's head. Underwood could feel it gathering around him, the fear and uncertainty running from man to man. And it was more than what was out there, but the fact that they no longer had any faith in Mac. He'd led them out here. He'd gotten them tangled up in this mess. And now that he had, he seemed to have no idea what to do next.

"You better come up with a plan," Underwood told him when they were out of earshot of the others. "These boys are looking to you for leadership. You can't let them down."

It looked as if Mac might take a swing at him, but after grinding his teeth a moment, he sighed. "I already got a plan, Pop, and that's getting the shitheads that killed Clayton and Corbett. You saw what they did. They chopped his goddamn head off."

Underwood swallowed. "And you think a man did that?"

"What else? A gator didn't bite his head off and then shove it on a stake."

"Gator wasn't what I was thinking."

Mac seized him by the shirt and backed him up against a tree. "And what were you thinking, Pop? What kind of crazy shit you got going through your brain?"

Underwood, who was known for his calm head and easy way, shoved

Mac back. "Knock it off. You might be the lieutenant of the guard, but I'm the goddamn sergeant. These men see us scuffling, your little rabbit hunt is all over with."

Mac was fuming—frustrated, angry, and probably scared to boot— but he took a deep breath. "We're in a fix," he admitted.

"Darn right we are," Underwood said. "And it's not going to get any easier. We haven't been able to raise the other search parties on the radio and we're too far into the Snakebit to raise the prison. We're lost out here and we're in danger. We need to think on that."

Of course, Mac knew what he was getting at: call it a day, pull out, let the dogs lead them out of the swamp. But that was the one thing he would never do and Underwood knew it. If he did that, it would mean failure. The shitheads had killed his guard, maybe killed Corbett, and he wasn't able to bring them to ground. A big ugly black mark on his record.

"We ain't lost. The dogs can get us out any old damn time."

"So let 'em do just that."

"Hell I will."

Underwood sighed. Pig-headed as always. Too damn proud to admit he was out of his league. He'd never give up or give in. And while those might have been admirable qualities under ordinary circumstances, out here they were just going to get men killed.

"So what's your plan?"

Mac pulled long and hard off his cigarette. "We're going after them. We're going to bring them in."

Underwood could barely contain himself. Of all the reckless, arrogant foolishness. He wanted to slap Mac down and tell him, really tell him, what a shitting punk he was. Not a lick of common sense or a single working brain cell. All he cared about was advancing his career and he didn't care how much blood he spilled. He could never wrap his feeble mind around the fact that there was something out here, something unnatural, and that it would kill them all as it had killed so many through the years.

*But he'd never believe you. You know that. Even if he saw the special file with all the names of the guards and cons and whatnot that disappeared out here, he'd never accept the fact that there was something in these swamps that hunted men. Never.*

And maybe he would have told him regardless, but at that moment Charney cried out and started shooting. Reflex action: the others joined in. In a split second, the tension had ramped up and released itself. Mac was yelling, but it did little good. Charney, Peters, and Keye were out of their heads, blazing away while Lofquist's dogs barked and howled, driven mad by the noise and the violence and sheer terror coming off the men.

"STOP IT!" Mac yelled. "GODDAMN YOU, STOP IT!"

But they were not stopping. They'd been under an unbearable strain of fear, paranoia, and apprehension for so long, that they were irrational in their need to let off steam. Action, any action, was like a pressure-relief valve. And it was wide open. Rifles were discharged, pistols emptied, bullets flying in every which direction. They were tearing up the foliage around them, shooting at shadows and trees and bushes, reloading, then doing it again. There was no stopping them until they got it out of their systems. Underwood went down into the grass because, sooner or later, somebody was going to get hit.

But not Mac: he waded right in, knocking weapons from hands and kicking men and shoving them down. And when Keye still didn't stop, he punched him in the face.

"Lieutenant, I—"

But Mac wasn't having that either: he hit him again and then again until Underwood pulled him off him. And even then, he was crazy with rage, arm cocked, fist ready to drill Underwood in the face.

"Enough, Mac," he said. "By God, that's enough."

By that point, the dogs were absolutely uncontrollable. They were snapping at each other, snarling at Lofquist, howling and whining. It was just too much for them. They were bloodhounds, working dogs, but with wolflike instincts at their core and they wanted to fight.

Everyone sat there, breathing hard, eyes wide and wet-looking like stunned cows. Keye was bleeding from the nose and mouth, continually touching his fingertips to his own blood as if he couldn't believe it had come out of him.

"I thought I saw something," Charney admitted. "I ... I saw a black shape. It was there. It was watching us. It had red eyes."

Despite the oppressive heat, Underwood felt a chill run up his spine. "Imagination," he said. "This goddamn place would scare anyone."

Peters had given Keye a handkerchief to stem the blood flow. "You shouldn't have hit him," he said to Mac. "That's one thing you should never have done."

Mac was going to go after him, too, but Underwood stepped in his path, holding his hands out to calm him. "Don't, Mac. We're in enough of a bind."

Mac looked at Keye, his mouth pulled into a scowl. "Goddamn amateurs," he said. "Not even men. Afraid of shadows like little boys. Pathetic."

Underwood knew him well enough to know that he'd never admit that he was wrong in hitting Keye. But everyone else knew it. That was the problem. They'd all seen it and they were all going to report it when they got back. Mac's dreams of advancement had just died an ugly death.

He got him away from the others because the chemistry between them was toxic now and the dogs were too damned loud.

"Mac, this is over. It's a damn mess and we have to call it a day before somebody gets hurt."

He was expecting Mac to go off on him, but he didn't. Instead, he stared up at the moon as if it mesmerized him. The bloated, full, glowing orb up there, studying them, watching them, peering down sardonically at the petty, pitiful affairs of men. It watched them ages ago when they were savages in animal skins and it watched them now, seeing very little difference.

Mac looked at the encroaching shadows, the misting swamps and shook his head. "Sorry, Pop. That shouldn't have happened. It should never have happened. I lost my cool same as they did. Unprofessional."

"Yes, it was. Now you have to think about repairing the damage."

"By giving up."

"Not giving up. Just getting out of here and regrouping. It's too damn dangerous out here at night. You have to see that."

"You really believe there's spooks out here."

"I didn't say that."

"You didn't have to."

Underwood sighed. "Listen to me. If those shitheads are within a mile of us, they heard the shooting, the dogs, the shouting. They're gone now. We have to get out of here and come back by daylight with enough men to do this job properly."

"You want me to call this off, go back and tell the warden that I failed, that I didn't do everything I possibly could to bring those killers in. That's what you want me to do."

Boy, this guy. Hardheaded as they came. "No, I want you to practice some common sense. The Snakebit is too big. We'd need hundreds of men to cover it properly and even so, Christ, it would take weeks if not a month. We're not equipped to handle this."

"Bullshit."

"Mac, c'mon. Pull us out of here. The men would respect you if you did that."

"I don't want their respect; I want them to act like men and follow orders."

"That's never going to happen now."

"It better or I swear to God, I'll kill them myself."

Underwood opened his mouth—something boiling inside him demanded that he do so—but then he closed it again, because there simply were no words to encapsulate how he felt about this man. Interestingly enough, old Mac was still staring up at the moon as if he was looking for spiritual guidance and not getting any.

Then a black cloud rolled over its face.

Underwood flinched as if he was expecting something else. Another cloud passed and the shadow it threw over the swamplands was menacing in its darkness. Then a black mass was drawn over it like a veil and it got really dark. The blackness seemed as thick as the weave of a blanket.

Somebody screamed with a shrilling volume and it was like a thousand fingernails dragged over a thousand blackboards. The dogs went silent, then they began to whimper and bay.

"What the hell?" Lofquist said.

Underwood smelled an overpowering death-smell that was pungent and sickening. His guts coiled in his belly and bile shot up the back of his throat. It stank the way he imagined the mold-speckled lining of a buried casket might smell. *This is it, this is really it,* a tiny voice whispered in his head. *It's about to show itself.* The clouds parted for maybe two seconds and in that brief span of time he saw that the sky was filled with swooping, hook-shaped forms, black and glistening, darting about like bats.

Then the clouds moved in again and the darkness swallowed them.

"What the hell is going on?" Mac said, shining his light around like the others, trying to capture something, *anything,* that would put this in some sane perspective. The stink had descended on them in a black cloud. There were flapping sounds above them like sheets on a clothesline in a high wind. Swooping noises. The dogs baying. The men crying out. Flashlight beams moving back and forth in shaking hands like searchlights.

The men started shooting again.

But this time, they were not just shooting into the shadows, but into the sky. In a muzzle flash, Underwood thought he saw a black, hairy wing, easily five feet in length, then it was gone. Something soared over his head with that hot, gaseous odor and his flashlight revealed a yawning mouth filled with overlapping yellow fangs and two beady red eyes burning in their intensity.

Men screamed and emptied their guns.

Mac was firing wildly, too, and the dogs were not baying now, they were whining in terror. One of them howled in pain. Then another. And another. In the perpetually strobing muzzle flashes, Underwood saw

Lofquist and it looked like he was covered in blood. He heard the dogs yapping in agony and the insane thing was it seemed to be coming from overhead. A mist of blood broke against his face. Guns were clicking on empty chambers. He saw Keye stand up and try to make a run for it, but he was cut down in the crossfire. Something like huge claws seized Charney and he was pulled up into the air like a mouse seized by an owl.

"INTO THE TREES!" he shouted at the men. "GET INTO THE FUCKING TREES!"

Then everyone was moving, stumbling into the protection of the pines, ducking under boughs and tripping over limbs, themselves, and each other.

Then silence.

Nobody moved. Nobody breathed. Nobody dared make a sound. Then, finally, those who still had flashlights clicked them on and Underwood got a look at who was left—Mac, Peters, and Lofquist. They were all spattered with whorls of blood. It was shining on their uniforms and streaked over their faces.

But there was silence.

Lights were shined out into the grass. They saw Keye's sprawled corpse out there on the blood-matted ground. It looked like he was floating in a pool of red ink. But the dogs were gone. It was a slaughter. No more, no less.

"My dogs," Lofquist sobbed. "Oh, my dogs ... I raised them from puppies ... I kept them, I cared for them, I trained them ... "

He kept sobbing like a spanked child, completely out of touch with reality. He was a tough man. Underwood had known him for years. It took a lot to break a man like him, but this had done it. He wanted to comfort him, but there was just no way to do it. No way.

Lofquist still had their leads in his hand and he pulled them toward him. Most were cut or split, but one was still attached to something. And as he yanked it forward, reeling it in like a fisherman, the men turned away, sick to their stomachs. One of the bloodhound's heads was still in the harness, eyes glazed, mouth hanging open, fur stiffening with drying blood.

"Jesus," Peters said. "Somebody ... somebody get rid of that thing."

But nobody had the heart to take it from Lofquist. He was no longer speaking out loud. Tears were rolling down his face and his mouth was moving, but no words came out.

"You happy now, Mac?" Underwood said. It just came out as he knew it would sooner or later.

"Hell you say?"

The moon had come back out again and both men were dappled in its light, the shadows of tree branches above laying across them like stripes of charcoal.

"We've got three dead men now. All on your watch. The dogs are gone. We have no way to get out of here and all because you didn't have a single lick of common sense. A goddamn snot-nosed little boy who couldn't admit that he was wrong and that he was in way over his head—"

Mac hit him. It was a good shot: powerful, quick, devastating. Underwood went down, blood on his mouth. Peters jumped to his feet and looked like he was going to go after Mac.

Underwood laughed and wiped his mouth. "Don't bother, son. Mac's all washed up and he knows it. His career is over. We get back to Stackhouse, he'll spend the next ten years cleaning toilets."

Mac just stood there, trembling, shaking with rage and failure and the hurtful knowledge that he turned a very bad situation into an atrocity. He bunched his hands into fists, hung his head, then chattered his teeth. Then something struck his face, a red drop that ran down the bridge of his nose. It was followed by another and another. He pawed them away with his hands. Peters played his light around in the branches overhead. High up there, maybe twenty feet or so, the carcasses of two bloodhounds were speared on limbs, completely impaled. They were split open, pink coils of intestines hanging from them like party streamers.

"My dogs," Lofquist said.

Mac stared up at them and then dropped to his knees, promptly vomiting into the grass.

Peters dropped his flashlight and Underwood just sat there, thinking about the poor damn dogs, wondering how long they had before they met the same fate.

<h2 style="text-align:center">-22-</h2>

Just like in the war, Pegg was tracking men again, tracking them in the darkness. And the smell and feel of the swamps brought all those night patrols back to him. That did not make him feel stronger or more confident. He was older now. He wasn't some empty-skulled young buck out to prove himself. He was older, calmer, more reasonable. And with age had come a sort of wisdom, at least, it had given him the ability to think things through, to remember his past and all that haunted it.

As he moved through the night, trying not to make too much noise, ruminating on what was and what had been, he suddenly became aware of something that stopped him dead.

It was a smell.

It was high and sweet, sickening. He breathed it in, wrinkling his nose. It made him ache between his shoulder blades from the old scar there where he'd been hung in the wreck of the plane in Pavuvu.

*But that didn't happen. Remember: they told you it was jungle fever. None of it really happened.*

The scar, however, told a different story.

And so did the sudden smell—because it was exactly like the plane smelled: like a hot envelope of decomposition. He tried to talk himself out of it, but something inside him refused to be swayed. It was definitely the same awful stench; there was no mistaking it. He remembered thinking that the inside of the plane smelled like the warren of a flesh-eating ogre, something that fed on human flesh and tacked the skins of its kills to the walls as trophies.

Something dropped onto his face and skittered toward his mouth. He slapped it away. Just a spider, but it made his flesh crawl. He remembered reading once that sometimes *they* could control nature, creating winds and storms to disable their prey, that they could command nature, make wolves and bats and spiders serve them.

*You're too old to believe in comic book shit like that.*

And how many times had he told himself that through the years, particularly at night when he woke up shaking, sweating from a nightmare of Pavuvu in his bunk. Too old, too adult, hell yes, he'd seen too much of the real world to believe in spooks and night crawlers, all that fairy-tale shit.

*But what about now? What do you believe in out here in this pestilent goddamn swamp ... Dog? Do you believe such things can be? That there are pallid, bloodsucking horrors, graveyard shadows that haunt the edges of civilization and feed on men and women and children? Do you believe now?*

He didn't ... yet, he *did*. His rational mind could reject it all it wanted, but his guts, his heart, his instincts knew better.

*They're here. Just like in Pavuvu. They lair in lonely places like this and they probably always have.*

Another spider dropped on his neck and another ran up his arm. He slapped the one away on his neck and seized the other on his arm between thumb and forefinger. In the moonlight, he could see its round, repulsively soft body and skittering legs. It seemed to throb the way a wound set with infection will. He tossed it aside. It was unnatural. He wondered for a moment if it was all in his head, but he took no chances; he darted out from the tree he was hiding under.

He licked his lips, he swallowed, he gripped the shank in his hand that much tighter.

The smell was suddenly stronger, almost as if it was not being carried on the air but being purposely directed at him. It filled his head, making his heart pound and his head whirl. The memories of Pavuvu were strung thick as webs in his head and he could not think his way around them. They seemed to own him at some very essential level, color him, describe him even.

He thought: *If it's them, if it's really them, if they really exist...it can't be the same ones. Not here. Not on Despair Island.*

But why not?

Why the hell not?

Pavuvu was an island, too. A world away, yes, but that world was shattered by war. Jungles flattened by bombing. Every ragged bush and pond and bamboo thicket fought over and painted with the blood of men. *They* had chosen Pavuvu because it was remote, sparsely populated, abundant with trackless forests in which they could breed and hide, issuing out only at night to seize prey. The same way that throughout history they had chosen lonely mountaintops, abandoned burial grounds, ruined desert cities, and dark forests. The places that would become inherent to their legend: lonely, windy wastelands.

He heard a squeaking sound.

It came from just above his head and his instinct immediately told him, *bat!*, even if his imagination told himself something else entirely. Whatever it was, it was small and swift. It zipped over his head, brushed the back of his neck. He slashed at it with the shank, missing entirely. And then it swooped too low and got its claws tangled in his hair. It squeaked and fought furiously. But by then, he had it in his hands, tearing out a clump of hair as he held it pinned to the ground by its wings.

Not a bat.

Dear God, it was no damn bat.

Not exactly.

He recalled the larval offspring hanging from the female's milk-swollen teats on Pavuvu … this was one of them, still immature, but wholly formed into the bloodsucking horror it would become. It kept making squeaking and hissing sounds. He could see it quite well in the moonlight—it was about the size of a puppy, its body rat-like with a whipping segmented tail, bones thrusting beneath gray, leathery skin bristled with hairs. Its wings were powerful. Its face was vaguely human-like, save its nose was the triangular depression of a skull. Its jaws were wide and fanged, its skin beady and gray-green like that of a lizard, its darting eyes red and translucent.

*Real,* he thought with terror as he struggled to keep it pinned. *A vampire. This is a fucking vampire.*

He knew if it got loose, it wouldn't just fly off like an ordinary animal. No, it would go right at him, impaling his throat with those long yellow fangs, opening his throat and bathing in his blood, sucking the life from him until it was too engorged to fly.

He let go of one wing and it nearly got loose—but he was too fast. He pulled the shank and jabbed it in the body two or three times in rapid succession until its thick, hot blood squirted over the back of his hand as its frantically-beating heart emptied its veins. Its struggles weakened and it stopped moving.

But Pegg was not satisfied.

He'd read those stories in *Weird Tales* when he was a kid, looked at the horror comic books that made the rounds in one lockup after another. So he sawed its little head off with the shank. Only then was he satisfied. He wiped the blood from the blade on his pants, then he held the head up so he could study it. Its pointed bat-ears were beginning to droop, eyes going pink as if there wasn't enough blood left in it to give them their vibrant hue. But its jaws were still open, oversized, upper and lower canines like yellow tusks.

He tossed it into the bushes with a cry of horror.

He struggled to his feet, but his knees were weak and his head was spinning. He stumbled forward maybe ten or fifteen feet, then went down to his knees again. He'd been so close to the thing that its venomous, musky stink had made his head spin. Now he breathed real air, fresh as it could be out in these rotting swamps.

*The stories,* he thought then, as he fished a home-rolled cigarette from the tin he kept in the pocket of his stripes, striking a match and lighting it. *All those stories.*

Sure, he'd heard them from day one at Stackhouse. Twice-told tales about cons escaping into the Snakebit never to be seen again. The hacks out hunting them sometimes never returned either. The old-timers said there were *things* out in the swamps that only came out at night. But in his naiveté, he'd always thought they were referring to monster gators. Maybe it wasn't so. Whenever you pushed those old hard cases, they clammed up. They never wanted to talk about it.

Maybe this was why.

He smoked and thought, letting the nicotine fire his brain and get the wheels rolling. He needed to let Pegg the convict die and start thinking like the old Pegg, the Marine Raider, if he wanted to survive out here. He still had to find the kid. That was paramount. And he had to sort out Drake. That was a necessity. But it was bigger than all that. Bigger than cops and dogs hunting convicts through the swamps. Much bigger than that. A point on the map a world away (Pavuvu) had suddenly connected itself to Despair Island and the darkest experience of his life was coming full circle to slap him right in the face.

He would find the kid.

And take care of business.

But along the way, he was going to have to kill himself some vampires. And this time, he wasn't leaving any of them alive to start a new colony.

## -23-

In the dirty moonlight, mist rose from the swamps like steam from a boiling stockpot. It drifted through the vegetation like the shrouds of ghosts. Gus could feel the heat of it, smell its rotten egg stink. He was crouched with the others beneath the spreading ferns, scared like he had never been before. Marrow-deep scared in a way that prison or shit-brained convicts like Drake could never, ever inspire.

*You're afraid for something precious inside you,* he thought then. *Maybe not your life force, but your soul.*

He hoped that the trackers would find them and end this nightmare already. Christ, even his cell sounded better than this. The cockroaches. The hacks. The animals crying out in their sleep.

Nobody had spoken in some time now.

Even Drake wasn't running his piss-hole of a mouth and trying to build himself up.

*Because he's scared like a little boy. That thing is going to come back and this time it might be for him.*

So they sat and they waited. Gus wished Pegg was there, because he would have known what to do. He always knew what to do. Drake and Swede weren't even in his class. They were just thugs. Dumb animals who'd ended up in a cage because of one stupid mistake after another. It was too tough to work for a living and actually accomplish something, so they'd taken what they wanted and society had punished them by taking their freedom. But in a situation like this you could see exactly what they were made of. He could smell the fear coming off them in a hot, sour stink. The way vermin smelled when they were cornered.

"How long we gonna wait here?" Swede finally asked.

"I don't know. Thing might still be out there."

"It's not," Gus said.

"And how would you know?" Drake asked.

"The smell. It has a smell when it comes. I can't smell it. It's long gone."

Drake spit into the undergrowth. "Then go out there, you little shit. Show me how brave you are."

Gus didn't want to, but at the same time he was going to just to expose Drake as the frightened little boy he indeed was.

"Okay. No sense sitting here pissing myself like you."

Swede giggled. Drake swore under his breath.

Though his knees felt like rubber and his guts were twisted into knots, Gus got up and pushed through the ferns. He made a big show of breathing in and out like he was sucking in fresh morning air and not the rank fetor of the marshes. He stepped over to a bush, his heart banging away in his chest, freed himself and urinated. Then, slowly, as if he didn't have a care in the world, he returned and sat down.

"There. See? No bogeyman."

"Kid's right. We need to get moving," Swede said.

Gus could feel the anger coming off of Drake. He'd been shown up by a punk bitch and that made him burn. But for all that, he made no moves on him.

"Hell with it," Swede said. "I gotta piss, too."

He stood up and walked over to where Gus had been, looking around warily. Gus smiled. He'd done it. He'd set him up. The thing was, he could still smell that sweet, sickening odor, it just wasn't as strong. But it was there. Just as the creature it came from was still there.

Drake stood up now, too, very carefully. He was definitely not as at ease as Swede. That much was obvious from his body language. He was a creature of instinct and his back was up. He wanted to believe it was safe, but he was certainly not convinced.

"I don't know," he said. "I think I still smell something."

"It's probably the shit in your pants," Gus told him, pushing it even further because he knew he had to.

Drake aimed a kick at him, growling in his throat … but his leg froze in mid-stride. Swede giggled as he relieved himself. That sweet stink was dialed from two to ten in a split second.

Gus, his breath locked in his throat like a fist was squeezing his windpipe shut, saw something in the darkness right next to Swede—a distorted, rising shadow, a monstrous form that seemed to be filling itself out as if it was inflating like a balloon. Swede was no longer giggling. In fact, he was no longer pissing. He was frozen up with terror as that shadow expanded right next him, snake-like and writhing with a terrible motion. It peered at him with bright green eyes that slowly turned a luminous pink.

"Oh, shit…" he managed to utter.

Then the thing moved.

It lashed out with its claws and Swede's throat was torn out, tissue and blood spraying into the bushes. He stood there, teetering drunkenly and stupidly, for maybe two seconds as the blood jetted from his throat. Then he folded up and went down.

Gus heard Drake pissing himself as he dropped to his knees. He whimpered like a child.

The creature spread its dark, membranous wings like a winding sheet and hovered over Swede. Then, like a gigantic bat, it crawled over him, its jaws opening to catch the jetting blood. Its mouth closed on the open artery and it began to make licking, slobbering, and sucking sounds, gulping down hot blood. As it did so, its beady eyes went from pink to bright red. It lifted its hideous bat-like face once and it was wet and dripping with blood. Then it fastened it to Swede's throat again, sucking hungrily, its body swaying back and forth with an almost sensual delight, quivering, its musculature quaking, its wings flapping slowly, its high pointed ears twitching.

It drained him that fast.

Then it put its scarlet eyes on Gus as if it knew exactly what he had done. How he had helped it feed. Gus sat there, holding back a scream, revolted by what he had just seen and what he had just helped to engineer.

The creature made a low purring sound like a satisfied cat that had just filled its belly with warm milk. It lifted one arm and he saw the hooked, triple claws on it that ripped out Swede's throat, the wing spreading beneath it, oily and shining, set with stray tufts of wiry hair.

A few feet away, Drake was sobbing, shaking, carrying on in a squealing, childlike voice: *"No ... no ... no, don't let it ... oh please Mama Mama Mama ... don't let it touch me ... please don't let it touch me..."*

Broken.

Absolutely broken.

And in the back of his mind, Gus realized that prisons were filled with abused little boys tormented by childhood traumas. And Drake—tough, throat-slitting, intolerant bully—was one of them and the terror of what he had just seen had launched him backward until he was just a scared boy again, crying out for the mother that had probably abused and abandoned him.

Gus didn't even look as heard wings flapping behind him. As something grabbed Drake and took him screaming up into the sky.

The creature that had drained Swede crawled closer and closer to him as bats crawl, dragging itself forward with its claws and bunched wings. He did not try to get away; they were behind him and flying overhead. If he panicked now, they would slaughter him.

His heart racing, his muscles convulsing with adrenaline, he watched it get closer and closer. When it was three feet away, it lifted its head, red eyes shining, its mouth opening until it grinned like a skull. It exhaled a cold breath of tombs in his face.

And then it seized him.

When he cried out, it laughed with the eerie, shrieking sound of a jackal.

## -24-

In the wee hours of the night, jittery from caffeine and nicotine, Warden Keafer sat in her office paging through the special file. It was either the most disturbing thing she'd ever read or the biggest pile of fiction imaginable. Her logical mind told her it was mostly the latter, a collection of superstition, campfire tales, and poor observations made by men who'd survived Snakebit Swamp (and not in the best condition).

But another part of her mind—the part that dreamed, imagined, fueling itself with instinct and premonition, that sometimes glimpsed dark conspiracies moving beyond the veil of reason—was not so sure.

*But it can't be. None of it can be.*

She lit another cigarette, her hands trembling, partly from stimulants and partly from the dressing-down she'd just gotten from the BOP in general and Franklin Blowden in particular. *I don't know what kind of half-assed dog-and-pony show you're running there, Margaret, but I suggest you clean your house right now. Get those inmates back in their cells. You've got a dead guard, escaped convicts, and search parties lost in a goddamned swamp. Straighten it out. If you don't, the newspapers will roast you alive and this time, I will not stand in their way. Wrap it up by morning or they'll be calling for your head.* Oh, yes. This was the big one: the career-ender. This was where all her critics became vindicated and all her friends stopped answering her calls.

She closed the file.

She locked it away.

She thought about McClaren and his search parties. She thought about Pegg and the other convicts. But mostly she thought about how she was going to weather the storm when everyone agreed that a prison warden was a man's job and she'd had no business in it in the first place. That irked her more than anything.

If the escapees and her guards could survive out there until morning, she might just have a slim chance of pulling this off.

But dawn was a long way off.

# THREE:

## BLOOD FEAST

### -1-

When Wiles opened his eyes, he was in the darkness. His wrists were bound above his head with rope or twine and from them he dangled. The more he struggled, the more he swung back and forth, the fibers digging into his skin.

*Make sense of this,* a voice said in the back of his head, trying to steer him from panic into reason.

There had to be a reason.

Something crawled over his face. He felt flies buzzing about his wrists.

*The swamp.*

Then it started to come back: Snakebit Swamp. The hunt for the escaped shitheads. Sgt. Teague. Corbett's death. All of it. And the more it came back, the more he felt his mind begin to crumble.

He began to squirm and thrash, which only made his plight that much worse as he swung from side to side, his wrists aching and his breath catching in his throat.

As his eyes adjusted to the gloom, he began to see shapes around him. Vague at first, they slowly took on detail until he realized that there were others hanging there with him, strung by the wrists. The very idea made him want to scream until his throat bled.

His mouth opened to do just that, but no sound came out save a dry rush of air. His heart pounded, his temples pulsed, his breath scraped in his throat.

He had never felt so helpless in his life because he knew that what had tied him and the others would be back. They had not been brought here for no reason.

*The flying things,* a voice whimpered in his mind. *The bat-things. You know what they are. They have a name. Say it.*

But he wouldn't because once he framed that old, terrible name; what was left of his mind would completely splinter. As it was, his brain was filled with imagery of ancient tomb-yards clustered on hilltops, riven graves, and night-black shadows that issued from the mouths of mold-encrusted sepulchers.

Now he could see more of what was around him. He was in some sort of attic or loft, crisscrossed rafters high above, gaping holes in the roof through which moonlight spilled in. He smelled age and rot and mildew.

And then it got worse: there was an overpowering stench of black soil, putrescence, and ... blood. Not fresh blood, but old blood. Copious spilled amounts of it that had dried to brown whorls. It smelled the way he imagined a closed-up slaughterhouse would stink: rank with the memory of blood, meat, rancid fat, and drainage.

Then—

*Listen.*

*Oh, dear God, listen.*

Something that had secreted itself in the shadows was breathing. He could hear it. It made a whistling, rasping sound that grew louder and louder as if it was excited by the fact that he was awake. It began to move in his direction ... worming, rustling ... as it dragged itself ever closer.

Now it was mere feet away, something that wore the shadows like a shroud. Its fetid smell was sickening. He could feel a sickly heat coming off it in waves. He saw a sort of pushed-in face with a heavy brow and protruding jaws, beady rodent's eyes that glittered in dark hollows.

And then it did the worst possible thing: it spoke. With a dry, crackling voice, a hissing expulsion of graveyard stink, it said, *"Wiiiiiiilllllleeeeesssss ... look at me ... Wiiiiiiilllllleeeeesssss..."*

Now he did scream with a wild, hysterical shrieking that blew out of his guts and the channel of his throat, echoing endlessly as his mind pulled into itself and went soft with rot.

By the time its fangs nipped his throat and its cold lips pressed over the wound and that awful sucking began, Wiles ceased to exist.

### -2-

The thing that dogged Teague, one of many, was that he couldn't honestly be sure if he was marching his men deeper into the swamp or out of it. There was just no way to know. The moon didn't seem like it was moving and he didn't have the time to sit around and wait for it to do so.

*If you don't get these boys out right now, you never will.*

And he knew that, God how he knew that. He was not naïve enough to believe the night-things would not return. This was their place, their hunting grounds, and he had inadvertently invaded it. The creatures would hunt them relentlessly, just as they had hunted other men that had made the mistake of coming into the Snakebit.

He led the way, moving carefully along land bridges that cut through the swamp, his remaining men behind him, moving single file. They were terrified and trigger happy and he did not like the idea of them being at his back with guns in their hands, but he had no choice. This was up to him now. Marco and Labonski would have scattered and run if he didn't keep barking orders at them and Suterman, well, he was simply broken, dragged along behind them like a toy on a string.

Teague thought: *Keep moving, keep going. Do not hesitate for a moment or you'll lose control of them. Do not think. Do not try to make sense of this.*

It was so much like walking night patrol in Korea that for a moment he could have believed he was a much younger man. But this was not Korea. It had been cold there, frost sparkling on the ground, but here it was hot and stifling, clouds of bugs swarming around you almost constantly. As scary as the nights were there, they always seemed to come to an end. But here in this goddamned swamp, night went on forever and ever.

"We're lost," Marco grumbled. "I've seen that same tree a dozen times. We're going in circles."

"We're fine," Teague told him, which had to be the biggest lie he'd ever told. "Just keep moving."

"No, I think he's right," Labonski said.

"I'm judging our position by the moon. It's all I've got. If we keep moving this way, it'll bring us out."

He tried to say that with complete confidence and complete conviction, because if they heard even a suggestion of doubt on his voice, he'd lose them.

"Keep quiet now."

He pushed ever forward, knowing it was going to take a lot more than determination to get them out of this. But if they could at least reach the very outskirts of the swamp itself, they'd have a fighting chance. And if fate favored them, maybe they'd bump into another search party... though in a wild area like this, some twelve or thirteen square miles in area, the chances were slim indeed.

*Mac got you into this mess,* he thought, *with his usual lack of foresight. That sonofabitch.*

Teague could easily feel the fear coming off Marco and Labonski. The atmosphere of the swamp had been initially menacing, but now it was positively sinister like an envelope of poison. It seemed to seep into every pore. He swallowed it with every breath. It lay inside him at his core in a black, malignant mass.

Every dozen feet or so, he paused, allowing his senses and instinct to catch up with him. He was relying on the latter as a sort of early-warning system because it was all he had.

They were moving through a stand of sawgrass that seemed as impenetrable as a bamboo thicket. The stalks were high above their heads, the ground soft with standing water.

Teague moved carefully, using the barrel of his .30-06 to part the grasses as he advanced. He kept expecting to see a set of red eyes revealed right before some leaping goblin shape ripped his throat open.

"We should've gone around this," Labonski grumbled.

"That would have taken too long," Teague explained.

The sawgrass stand was immense. Along with some sickly-looking locust trees, it occupied the only convenient landmass bridging the open water and bottomlands. If they went around, it would have taken them easily an hour out of their way.

Marco's idea had been to secure some high ground and wait for dawn. It made sense. And under ordinary circumstances, Teague would have agreed.

*But you know those damn creatures won't allow it. If you sit still, they'll pick you off one by one.*

Because they were out there.

And they were watching.

Teague could feel their eyes crawling along the nape of his neck. They were relentless: staring, studying, scrutinizing their prey the way owls scrutinized mice and voles moving through a midnight field.

As he pushed through the sawgrass, it had an unnerving habit of closing up behind him. And more than once as he waited for Marco and the others to join him, there had been unpleasant moments of silence when he thought he was alone and they had been taken.

But the grass had to end; it couldn't go on forever.

And then it did. He parted it with his rifle and moved into a clearing, nearly going right on his face as he stepped into a shallow pond that came up to his ankles. Ahead, the ground was higher with hillocks of scrub, spreading bushes, and rank undergrowth. He saw alien-looking, moss-draped bald cypresses out in the marshes, drifting patches of mist, but not much else.

They could have been less than a mile from the swamp's outer edges or five miles into the depths of it for all they knew.

Behind him, Marco emerged from the grasses.

"Thank God," he said.

Labonski followed suit. He stumbled five feet from the stand and sat on a stump, brushing webs from his face.

Teague waited, the tension inside him rising like lava up the cone of a volcano.

"Where's Suterman?" he said.

Marco just stared blankly in the moonlight.

"He was right behind me," Labonski told them. "I could hear him right behind me."

Teague clicked on his flashlight and went back into the stand, following their broken path of fronds for thirty, then forty feet. He found not so much as a drop of blood. Suterman was gone and he wondered for how long. Had it been Suterman behind Labonski or something else entirely?

When he got back out, he clicked off his flashlight to save batteries. "I told you to keep an eye on him."

Labonski just shrugged. "He was there. I swear he was there."

"Do you want us to help you look, Sarge?" Marco asked.

But Teague just shook his head. "No, you idiots have done enough."

## -3-

Pegg knew one thing: in a fight for survival, in a war of attrition, victory favored the combatant who was most prepared for any eventuality. That was a keystone of Marine Raider training—always be prepared to fight and be motivated to win at all costs. Be ready to think on your feet, to change tactics at a moment's notice, and use whatever terrain nature offered to your advantage. In the island campaigns, the Japanese understood that. They used the terrain, preparing battlefields beforehand to favor their own forces.

Now there wasn't a lot that Pegg could do about the terrain, so he engineered his mindset to be ready for action at any moment. And since he knew his enemy (at least as well as any living man), he took into consideration their strengths: they could fly, they were physically strong, and they were extremely cunning.

But they also had weaknesses like any enemy.

They couldn't tolerate brightness or direct sunlight. They saw humans as prey, not equal combatants. That's how he had killed the male in Pavuvu, by exploiting its arrogance and its belief that he would die without putting up a fight. Their kind had always overwhelmed human beings with horror, paralyzing them with it.

If you wanted to kill them, you had to overcome that. You had to draw them in.

And if they didn't come to you, you went to them.

Pegg figured his mission was clear: he had to find Gus and nothing was going to stop him. *Nothing.*

He'd already discovered Carney's remains and he'd tracked the others through the swamp to the oasis of fern-covered high ground. And there he'd found Swede, perforated by fang punctures and bled white.

But no Gus.

No Drake.

The trail went cold there. Which, in Pegg's thinking, meant they had been taken away somewhere. Probably to a lair much like the one the vampires had in Pavuvu in the crashed airliner. Out there, somewhere, in a cave or a grotto, they had a nest. Drake and Gus would be there, hanging with others in a living blood bank.

But where?

The Snakebit was a big place. Realistically, it could take days or weeks to locate it, if it could be located at all.

Yet, as he sharpened willow branches into deadly stakes with his shank, he knew he would find it. His instincts would guide him there unfailingly. In his gut, he was certain he already knew the way.

But it was more than that.

He could feel it in every fiber of his body.

During the war, he'd developed a sort of sixth sense where the enemy was concerned and it had led him to them again and again. And now he was feeling the same way about the vampires.

*They know you're coming.*

*They want you to come.*

Yet, he didn't think it was *they* so much as *she.* The female from the war. She was the leader of the colony and she remembered him. Remembered that he had killed her mate and she wanted her pound of flesh.

He knew he was supposing a lot, but on some level, it all rang true.

*Think about it. Just think about it.*

The war had destroyed their secret lair on Pavuvu like everything else. Before that, it might have been in Europe or Asia. Who could say? They'd probably laired everywhere at one time or another, places where they were still remembered with folktales and vampire lore. After Pavuvu, they roamed again. Maybe island-hopping to the Americas or making the trip in the dark hold of a freighter.

Now they were here.

Now Pegg was here.

The strange machinations of fate had brought them together again and she knew it. And if he accepted that—and he did—then much of it made sense. Drake and the others had been carefully corralled and pushed closer to the lair with every attack. They had been the bait used to draw him to her.

They would meet again.

And this time, one of them would die.

Pegg finished his stakes, then he lit a cigarette, smoking it slowly and with great relish like a man facing a firing squad. Then he stood up, letting his instincts and sixth sense take over.

It was time to begin the journey to where she waited.

## -4-

Mac decided that he'd never forgive them for this godawful mess. He'd never forgive a single one of these shitting, gutless rat bastards for what they had done to him. Not Keye or Charney for dying or Lofquist and his worthless mongrel dogs, and certainly not Underwood for fragmenting the ranks or Peters for being his wide-eyed little tagalong.

Mac had offered the lot of them real leadership and the chance to be men, *real* men, for the first time in their miserable lives.

And how did they repay him?

With treachery.

By being cowards and mama's boys that were afraid of their own shadows, afraid to follow a real man to real victory. Had they listened to him, did what they were told to do when they were told to do it, they would have had those shitheads by now. They'd be going back to a heroes' welcome instead of stumbling back in, weary and beaten, goddamn failures.

They'd ruined themselves.

And they'd ruined him now, too. Taken away his career, his dignity, and his position as captain of the guard which was rightfully his.

*And they'll pay for it,* Mac thought. *Swear to God, somehow, they'll pay for it.*

He didn't know how. Not yet.

But there was a way and he planned on finding it before this night was through.

"Mac, there's something up ahead," Peters said.

But Mac had already seen it. In fact, he wondered if he hadn't been seeing it since they entered the clearing. In the moonlight, it looked oddly like a series of totem poles arranged on a low hilltop. He stood there, staring at them in the distance, a peculiar feeling spreading out in his gut, an inexplicable buzzing in the back of his head.

Nobody moved toward whatever it was.

But Mac, of course, wasn't surprised at that. These weren't real men with him. *Fucking Girl Scouts. Nancy boys.* There wasn't a collective ball between them. They would have stood there, he knew, shivering and pissing yellow in their boots for the rest of the night if he let them. They were waiting for him to take the initiative. Then they would follow at a distance, cowering in his shadow.

*Next, I'll be changing their diapers.*

Though he was scared inside, he wasn't about to let these meatheads see it. He'd sort this out, whatever it was. Because that's the kind of man he was.

He handed his riot gun to Peters. "Don't worry, boy. It's empty. It can't hurt you." Then he pulled his .38 and, long-barreled flashlight in hand, he began moving in the direction of the hill.

"You might want to be careful," Underwood warned him.

"The day I take your advice, Pop, will be the day I wear a skirt."

Surprisingly, Lofquist went with him. He did not speak. His eyes were glazed, his movements wooden. But for all of that, at least he was more of a man than the others. And that counted for something in Mac's book.

They climbed the hill together and when they got to the top, their flashlights revealed what was up there in grisly detail. Definitely not totem poles.

"Jesus," Mac said.

Lofquist kept scanning his light over the objects, making wet smacking sounds with his mouth. "It … it ain't my dogs," he called back to Peters and Underwood.

If Mac hadn't been so sick to his stomach at that moment, he might have laughed at the macabre humor of his statement. But there was nothing funny about what was on the hilltop—the carcasses of four men. One of which, Mac saw, was Sergeant Millhaus who'd been leading the third search party.

The four of them had been impaled on long stakes driven deep into the ground. The stakes had been shoved up between their legs and were dark with drying, sticky gore. Three of them had been disemboweled, their viscera hanging from their bellies in coils and tangles like fleshy, mating worms. Their faces were splattered with blood, eyes gouged out along with most of the orbits that had housed them, mouths sprung open as if they had died in mid-scream.

And they probably had, Mac figured.

Millhaus' face was dotted with meat flies. What looked like a swollen blue-black snake hung from his jaws. But on closer inspection, Mac saw (as warm bile squirted up the back of his throat) that it was his tongue. It had been savagely wrenched from his mouth. Not ripped out, but damn close.

By that point, Peters and Underwood had joined them. One look at the atrocity was enough for Peters, who turned away, coughing and gagging. Underwood stood his ground, though.

When he spoke, his voice was dry and wounded-sounding. "Bob Millhaus. Oh, Christ." He swallowed. "George Parradine." He swallowed again. "And that one...I think it's Frank Creek."

But it was hard to tell: his face looked like it had been flayed to the bone by a three-pronged garden trowel. Pink meat had pushed from the gashes and ruts like fresh mince.

As he turned to the fourth man, muttering, "Phil Brotherton," under his breath, the corpse moved. It jumped like a frog's leg when an electrode is inserted into the muscle.

Mac let out a cry, seized by a mindless, irrational terror. *Dead don't move. They...they can't move.* But he quickly recovered himself, though the corner of his mouth twitched with an involuntary tic.

"He ain't dead," Underwood said. "He ain't quite dead."

And he wasn't...though how he was even that much alive was anyone's guess. He convulsed again, teetering back and forth on the stake. By luck or design, the stake had missed an artery. His lips opened with a sticky sound. He breathed. His eyes, which had not been gouged out like the others, rolled back white in their sockets.

It was then that they noticed that a section of his cranium was missing as if something had taken a bite out of his head, not just tearing the scalp free, but a fist-sized portion of skull and brain. Blood and globs of gray matter had leaked from the chasm.

"*Ooooooohhhhh ... ooohhhh ... nooo ... noooo,*" he said in a deranged, moaning voice that rose and fell in a shrill squealing.

"Make it stop," Peters said. "Oh God, make it stop."

And then it finally broke up into a discordant noise that was somewhere between icy, mad laughter and a scream. Brotherton's mind was completely gone. He was brain-damaged, reduced to a wailing vegetable that shuddered on the stake that held him aloft.

Mac had never seen or heard anything so disturbing. It was eerie and pitiful at the same time. Sweat coursed down his face and it looked as if his eyes might pop right out of his head. He couldn't take it. As Brotherton continued to shriek louder and louder with that unearthly voice, Mac let out a manic cry and put two bullets into his forehead, blasting his skull apart.

"MAC!" Underwood shouted. "WHAT THE HELL ARE YOU DOING?"

But the thing was, he didn't know. He really didn't know. He wasn't even aware of pulling the trigger. He wasn't consciously aware of anything until he heard the report of the .38. And even then, he couldn't stop himself from jerking the trigger again. Something in his mind had snapped. The sight and, much worse, the *sound* of Brotherton had just been too much.

"You murdered him," Underwood said.

"I…I put him out of his misery."

"His brain was destroyed," Peters said. "He was suffering."

Underwood swallowed. "It's not our place to make that determination," he said, but with less conviction.

Lofquist just stood there, unmoved by any of it.

Mac couldn't take any more of it. He had to get away from them. He didn't like how they were looking at him, the way they judged him, the way their eyes burned into him. The stinking sonsofbitches had no right to look at him like that. He was in command. He was in charge.

How dare they.

*How dare they.*

Inside, he was raging and confused. If he didn't get away from the backstabbing bastards, he was going to do something terrible to them. So, he walked down the hillside where he could be alone, where he could breathe and make sense of things.

They were watching him, but he didn't give a shit. Let them. They didn't understand the responsibilities that came with command. He was only watching out for them, protecting them and the unity of his command. Why couldn't they see that? Why couldn't they simply … obey?

And it was at that moment, a moment of great revelation for him, that the weird buzzing in the back of his head grew in intensity like a drill bit whirring in his brain. He wanted to scream. But he didn't.

No, he *listened.*

Because a voice, a smooth, silky female voice was speaking in the depths of his mind.

*They betrayed you.*

*You showed them the way.*

*You watched over them.*

*And still they betrayed you.*

"Yes," Mac said. "That's it exactly."

*They need to be punished.*

"They do."

*Bring them to us. Let us punish them.*

Mac shook his head. That voice. He could not listen to that beautiful, terrible voice. Yet, he nodded, hearing exactly what he needed at that moment.

"But I don't—"

*Yes, you do.*

*You're going the right way. You're coming to us.*

*We're waiting at the end of the trail.*

*We'll punish them for you. We'll make them suffer. They'll scream. They'll bleed. They'll beg for mercy and you can watch every moment of it. With us.*

Then the voice was gone and he understood. For the first time in hours, he felt strong. He felt confident. He had a guardian angel now and the idea of that did not seem as crazy as it should have.

"Mac? What the hell are you doing?" Underwood called down to him. "Get up here."

"I know the way now."

"What?"

"C'mon, goddammit. I know the way. I know where the trail leads."

The three of them joined him and he led on, his sheep lined up obediently behind him as he brought them to the wolves.

### -5-

Mama was a small woman in wire-framed glasses, a smirk deeply etched onto her mouth as if she had seen the worst life had to offer and was not surprised by any of it. Maybe that's why she drank. And maybe that's why she was so mean sometimes.

As Drake listened to her droning voice—he didn't dare tune her out; the cigarette burns on his arms were testament to what happened when he did *that*—she moved in closer, her eyes dark and huge and scary.

"Do you know what your father was?" she asked him, sipping her vodka straight from a water glass. "He was a *bad* man. A very bad man. That's why he left us. That's why he never came home that night. He hated us, so he made us suffer. Do you understand that?"

Drake nodded, his eyes filled with tears.

"And do you know what you are?" she asked. "You're just *like* him. You'll grow up to *be* him. Don't deny it or you'll make me mad. You don't want me mad...do you?" She laughed with a sound like a knife scraping rust from metal. "One day, you'll grow up and you'll have a wife and a son and you know what? You'll leave them. You'll leave them in the cold to suffer. No money. No food. They'll have to live in a shack like we do."

Drake blinked his eyes. Mama liked to be mean to him. She liked to lock him in the attic where the bats squeaked and flew in through the hole in the roof. It didn't matter how much he cried or begged; she wouldn't let him out. But never had she tied his wrists like this and hung him from a rafter with rope and let him swing back and forth. Already his wrists were getting numb, the skin chafing.

She sat there watching him, her eyes huge behind her glasses as he sobbed and whimpered. She lit a cigarette and blew on the cherry until it was glowing hot.

"Bad boys become bad men. Haven't I told you that? Haven't I told you that again and again?"

She had. Oh, yes, she had told him lots of things. Men were snakes, poisonous snakes, that couldn't wait to sink their venom-dripping fangs into unsuspecting women and plant their terrible seed inside them. And once that was done, then they left, because their job was done and it was time to seek another woman because that's how the game was played. And she told him he had to be sent to the attic so he could think about who he was and what he was because one day he would be an evil predator like his father. She also told him that if he was quiet up there, really, really quiet, then the bats would leave him alone. But if he made too much of a fuss, they would tangle in his hair with their tiny claws and flap their wings in his face and bite his throat and give him rabies.

Often, when she was angry, her face would change, becoming a horrible grinning mask, but it had never been this awful before.

"Mama," he sobbed. "Stop changing ... oh please, *stop changing* ... "

But that only made her change more until her face was that of a bat—the sunken cavity where her nose should have been, the gray, rugose face, the gleaming red eyes with tiny black pinprick pupils, and the yawning, ever-widening cavity of her mouth with its pink, speckled gums and gigantic yellow teeth. She spread huge wings and clicked her deadly claws together.

*"Oh please, Mama, no ... no ... "*

By then she was closer, her hot charnel breath making him gag, her teeth puncturing his throat until the blood began to run. She wrapped her wings around him and they were hot and fuzzy, lice jumping on them. Then her mouth was fastened to his neck and she began to suck his blood with a slow, liquid slurping sound.

And it was as this ultimate violation occurred that Drake tried to scream, then his mind cleared for a moment and he remembered that he was no longer a boy and this place was not the attic of his childhood home and this abominable thing sucking his blood was surely not his mother.

-6-

Underwood had a very bad feeling and its source seemed to be Mac. Oh, Mac wasn't exactly a leader on a good day, but now his mind was going soft as a carved pumpkin two weeks past Halloween. He could tell himself it wasn't so—*oh hell, it's just goddamned Mac, you know how he is, he ain't like most people anyway*—but that wasn't gaining any traction under the circumstances.

*So you're gonna keep following him? Is that what you're going to do?*

He didn't know. Mac was certain he knew the way out and he was leading them there. Peters seemed to believe him. Lofquist was out of his head over the death of his dogs. And that left Underwood himself. His gut instinct told him that Mac was not leading them out, but deeper into the secret world of the Snakebit. Yet, he followed him. They all followed him.

Human optimism.

That's what it was. Even when you knew something was wrong or it didn't feel quite right, you went ahead with it and you believed what was served up to you because you *needed* to believe that everything would work out fine, that it would be just fine and peachy in the end. If it wasn't for that defect of the human mind, politicians wouldn't have a job and businessmen wouldn't be rich and young men wouldn't sign up to fight in wars.

He watched Mac moving through the shadows. His step was sure, easy, like a scout leader taking his pack down a well-trodden path. He seemed to know where the mudholes were, easily avoiding clusters of roots, and steered them around pools of open water.

*It's like he knows.*

But Underwood didn't think that was it. In fact, what he thought was that Mac was being controlled. Like a dog being led forward on a leash.

120

"Mac," he said. "None of this looks familiar. Not at all."

"You have to have faith," Mac told him.

And that was the last thing in the world the old Mac would have said. It would have been something more like, *Nobody's fucking asking you, Pop. Do what you're told or you're going on report.* No, this was all wrong and Underwood knew it, yet he was still following along as if his legs were carrying him on and he had no say in the matter.

Then he did stop.

So did Lofquist.

Even Peters stopped dead as if a hand had grabbed him.

That sweet-foul stench of putrescence, of moldering hides, filled the air. And as it did, they heard the sound of wings above them, flapping and soaring as shapes swooped over their heads. A dark mass came wheeling out of the sky, end over end, barely missing Lofquist. When it hit the ground (and it struck with amazing velocity as if it had been dropped from 500 feet up), it literally exploded—a bag of bones and meat and spraying fluid.

Lofquist let out a mad scream because it was one of his dogs. Its remains were splattered all around him, its drainage dripping down his face like streaks of motor oil.

They were in a clearing and Mac was standing near the tree line, not doing anything but watching. Underwood saw that and it disturbed him greatly in those two or three seconds before another carcass was dropped, this one winging Peters and knocking him flat before it hit the ground and erupted like a water balloon.

A third and fourth dog came down, each one with more speed than the last.

And then it was over with.

Peters and Underwood pawed dog anatomy and clumps of fur from themselves. Peters, still stunned, got drunkenly to his feet, made it two or three steps and slid on a greasy coil of dog intestines and down he went again, right atop a carcass, his arms sinking into its broken, jellied mass right up to the elbows. Underwood yanked a slimy ribbon of flesh from his hair and realized it was an eye stalk with a dangling optic nerve. He tossed it aside, saying *"Ugh,"* under his breath.

Lofquist was completely beside himself. It had all been bad enough, but this ... this was a fucking atrocity and he lost it. He took up his .30-30 Winchester and started blasting away at the sky, not aiming, just firing randomly until he ran out of shot. And even then, he kept levering and pulling the trigger, swearing and shrieking.

And Mac said, "Of all things. It's raining goddamn dogs."

And Lofquist charged him.

He moved too fast for Underwood to intervene, not that he planned on doing so anyway. Lofquist went right after Mac and Mac let him come. When he was six feet away, Mac pulled his .38 but he never had to use it. Lofquist ran right past him as if he saw something in the distance, something that had killed his beloved bloodhounds.

Underwood cried out for him to stop.

But Lofquist vanished into the shadows and it was less than a minute later that they heard him scream like an animal being put to death.

## -7-

When Gus opened his eyes, he did not know where he was or how he came to be there. There was just a distorted vision of flying through the sky that played over and over again in his head.

He heard a sound.

It wouldn't have been a terrible sound ordinarily, but in this dark place it made his skin crawl: a sucking. A sucking sound. And as he heard it, he realized his wrists were bound above his head and that he was hanging off the floor by them.

Like a sacrifice.

*They had him.*

*The creatures had him.*

And as he thought that, he could feel their minds crawling inside his own, cold, reptilian presences that slithered through his brain, examining his thoughts and memories, touching them, reading them, smelling them and *tasting* them.

"Stop it," he said, without meaning to. *"GET OUT OF MY HEAD!"*

And as he shouted that out, the sucking sounds stopped. There was a dreadful silence. The world became a vacuum. Then he heard a low, childlike whimpering followed by a shrill, insane voice saying, *"Oh, Mama, please no more ... no more ..."*

Drake.

He was certain it was Drake. Drake reduced to the level of a scared, abused little boy as he had been when that ... that *vampire* had drained the blood out of Swede. Yes, then they had taken them both away, to this place, this nightmare lair. Now it all made a certain amount of sense and Gus almost wished that his mind had remained blank. He saw the rotting timbers high overhead, the sections of missing roof, the moonlight shining down in dirty yellow beams.

Now the sucking sounds began again and somewhere he heard squeaking noises, the fluttering of many wings, and an unpleasant hissing/whispering.

*They know you're awake.*

*And when they're done with Drake, they'll come for you.*

It would have been easy to panic at that moment, to completely lose his mind and descend into childhood terrors like Drake, but Gus didn't. Maybe he wasn't tough on the outside, just terribly average, but he'd been through enough shit in his life that he had a resilience and fortitude on the inside that sometimes surprised even himself. He remembered Pegg saying to him, *Prison's full of bullies. Big guys that are tough on the outside because they're weak on the inside. Saw it in the war. Big guys who bragged about how tough they were. They were trying to convince themselves that it was true. But you know what? It was horseshit. When the rounds started flying and men were dying, they'd cry for their mommies. But little guys and ordinary Joes, the sort that were tough on the inside, they became warriors. Real warriors. Big muscles don't make you tough, kid. They just give you armor to hide behind so nobody can see how really gutless you are.*

The words played through his head and as they did so, Gus decided he could either die like Drake or he could go out like Pegg: fighting to his last breath.

With that in mind, feeling a confidence swelling inside him that had no reason being there, he began testing the strength of the rope that bound his wrists. It wasn't all that tight and with the sweat—and blood—coming from his wrists as a lubricant, he began to worm himself free. Slowly, carefully, with extreme caution and patience.

### -8-

Now fate began to favor Pegg as if he was on some kind of holy mission. It began to give him the things he needed so he could do the job at hand. As whatever was inside him showed him the path that would bring him to the place he needed to go, he discovered a stray boot in the grass. Upon seeing it, he knew it had belonged to a guard. One of those soft-soled prison boots they wore so they could sneak around at night without you hearing them.

He picked it up, examining it.

The foot was still in there, a bloody knob of bone protruding from it. He tossed it aside. Five minutes later, he found an arm that had been violently torn from its shoulder socket. The hand still gripped a .38 Police Special. Diligently, Pegg began the gruesome task of snapping the stiffening fingers from the weapon. Only one round had been fired. He slid it into his pocket.

A few minutes later, he found the torso of the guard. It had been split from crotch to throat like a paper doll cut by scissors. Its entrails were strung from its belly into the branches of a tree leaning over it. He searched the pockets of its bloodstained uniform shirt but found nothing of interest.

Then, a few yards away, he found a rifle. A .30-06 Springfield. Same rifle he'd used often in the war. He checked the load. Four rounds. He would have to make each one pay. He slung it over his shoulder by the strap.

He searched around for more weapons, but found nothing.

Now he would bring his kind of war to the vampires.

### -9-

It was Underwood who found Lofquist's remains. Mac and Peters didn't even bother accompanying him, so he went at it alone and he found them at the edge of a misting pool of black water; in fact, he tripped right over them. Lofquist had nearly been ripped in half, his blood sprayed easily five feet in every direction. Underwood slipped on it and came down on his corpse which seemed to break apart beneath his weight like a soft-boiled egg.

With a cry, he pulled himself free of it, gore all over his hands and uniform pants. The flashlight in his hand showed him Lofquist's face in grisly detail: the horror-struck eyes, the mashed nose, jaws open so wide it was as if the tendons had snapped.

He backpedaled out of the splatter zone, but he'd never get that sweet, coppery smell of blood out of his head. He tried to call out for the others, but his voice was lodged in his throat and stuck in his mouth. It seemed to have the consistency of maple syrup.

He sat there on his ass, shaking his head from side to side as if that might clear the horror—and the stink—from his mind when the convulsions began. He'd seen a lot up to that point and he'd kept his stomach down.

But this was too much.

He started vomiting and he couldn't seem to stop. The half-digested remnants of last night's meatloaf came up along with the side of peas and potatoes he'd eaten with it. After that, bile and water. And even then, emptied right out, he gagged until he coughed and finally, finally the convulsions ended.

By then, miraculously, Mac and Peters had showed up. Peters, of course, turned away, but Mac just stared at what Underwood's flashlight revealed in the grass. He swatted away skeeters and lit a cigarette very calmly, like a guy on his lunch break without a care in the world.

"He wasn't right since his dogs got taken," he said, tapping a finger to his temple. "Not right up here where it counts."

For not the first time, Underwood wanted to punch Mac right in the nose, but he knew that wouldn't do because Lofquist hadn't been the only one who was crazy. Mac was right off the map. Something in him, the part that made him a human being and a man, had been scrubbed away like a math problem on a blackboard. It was just … gone. Underwood looked from Lofquist's glazed eyes to the staring dead orbs of Mac and for one head-reeling, mad moment, he thought he heard voices in his brain, dry and scratching voices that he knew were the voices—or the *thoughts*—of the bat-things that were preying upon them.

*He belongs to us now.*

*We'll use him as we see fit.*

*And when he brings you to us, we'll break you like we broke the others because your kind are our sheep, our cattle, our livestock. You exist to feed us. Your blood is our wine—*

"Vampires," he said out loud, surprising even himself.

That word made Mac take one, then two faltering steps back. His hand shook as he dragged from his cigarette. "Vampires, you say? Like Lugosi and that kind of stuff? I watched those movies when I was a kid. Sure, but they ain't real. Ain't no such thing as vampires. I don't believe in that stuff."

"Don't you?"

It was not a question so much as an accusation and Peters seemed to pick up on it, as if maybe he'd been thinking along those lines himself.

"We better go," Mac said.

"Yes, we're expected, aren't we?"

"Don't know what you mean."

Underwood got to his feet. "They got you like a dog on a fucking leash, don't they? How many of them are there? And just what did they promise you?"

"Just shut your mouth," Mac said, walking away, taking up his trail again.

Peters looked from Mac's retreating form to Underwood. "What do you mean about vampires? Why you talking about crazy shit like that? Make-believe stuff. Spook stories. It's not funny. None of it's funny at all."

"No," Underwood said, turning and following Mac. "It's anything but funny."

## -10-

Teague knew they were being stalked carefully and quietly long before the others were aware of it. Whoever it was, he was good. Only stepping when they did, stopping at the same time, using the shadows as camouflage. Every time he looked back, this other was not there. Maybe Marco and Labonski couldn't sense him—or *it*—but Teague had spent too many dark nights in Korea listening for communist insurgents trying to sneak up on American positions not to be aware of it.

In his thinking, it was a man following them. Not one of the creatures. They were getting a little closer all the time. It came down to one of two things: either he waited for this mysterious other to show or he told Marco and Labonski and they went to ground. He decided on a third alternative.

"Let's take five. Get off our feet for a few minutes."

The others were all for that. They dropped into the dewy grass, breathing hard, wiping sweat and smashed insects from their faces.

Teague crouched down with his rifle and waited. Now whoever was out there would have to inch their way in. That's what he wanted. If he could draw a bead on them, he knew he could hit them.

But as he prepared for that, he thought, *you know damn well who it is. There's only one guy out in this goddamn swamp tonight who can move like that. One guy with that sort of training.*

Finally, he sighed, and called out, "Come in, Pegg. I know it's you."

Marco and Labonski had their guns up and were looking in every direction.

"Relax," Teague told them. "If he wanted to kill us, we'd be dead by now."

To his surprise, the brush rustled behind him. That sonofabitch had flanked them, snuck around them without making a sound.

"Got you in my sights, boys, so don't do anything stupid. I just want to talk. I just want us to survive this night."

"Lower your weapons," Teague ordered, lowering his own as well.

Pegg stepped out of the shadows in the ragged, dirty remains of his state stripes. He squatted down about five feet from Teague. "We been through the shit, ain't we? Hunted near to extinction by the vampires. And it ain't dawn yet."

"Vampires," Marco said. "Vampires."

"Good a name as any, son. They got wings. They don't like the light. And they drink blood. That name'll do just fine, I think."

"Where's the others you broke out with?" Labonski asked, apparently uneasy having a chat with this guy.

Teague understood that. They were supposed to be bringing him in. But extraordinary situations required extraordinary measures.

Pegg explained that they were supposed to meet up with him after the escape, but they never did. "Carney and Swede are dead. I found their bodies...or what was left of them. Drake and Gus are still alive, far as I know."

Marco said, "One of you killed Danny Clayton. You wanna deny that?"

Teague bristled. Now was not the time for that and definitely not the situation.

Pegg sighed and swore under his breath. "Well, it wasn't me. I got along with him okay. I don't think Carney or Swede would have done that. Definitely not the kid."

"Drake," Teague said.

"That'd be my guess."

Marco shrugged. "So says you."

"I think you know me better than that."

Teague decided to redirect things. There were more pressing matters. "So now what?"

"I know what's been killing your people and mine. I've come up against them before."

Pegg had their attention now, so he told them about what he'd done in the war, what happened at Pavuvu. He left no detail out.

"So what are they doing here?" Marco wanted to know.

"That would take a lot of guesswork that we don't have time for," Pegg told him. "I know where they are. I'm willing to bet that they're holding Drake and Gus, probably more than a few of your own people. If we don't get to them by dawn, they'll kill 'em."

"And how do you know that?" Labonski asked.

"I don't have the time to explain. We need to go get them now. If we do this together, we might have a chance."

"And we're supposed to take the word of a convict on that?" Marco asked.

"Easy," Teague told him.

"Don't see what choice you have, boy," Pegg said. "You can come with me and kill them or they'll kill you one by one."

Labonski cleared his throat. "The Sarge killed one of them."

Pegg looked over at Teague. "That true?"

"Got it in the head."

"Nice shooting. Now we need to go after them. You'll get a chance to kill some more."

Teague considered it. "All right. Let's go."

Marco and Labonski just looked at each other. They'd been through a lot. What Teague wanted them to do would put them through a lot more.

Pegg said, "If we wait for dawn, they're going to kill us. They won't let us live. They can't *allow* us to live. We need to bring the fight to them. It's our only chance."

"And maybe you're leading us into an ambush," Marco said.

"Maybe. But if I wanted to kill you boys, it would have been easy. I'm going. I want you to come with me. Either way, I'm going."

"Let's do it then," Teague said.

### -11-

When Gus dropped to the floor, it was not with the stealth he'd hoped for. His knees hit the planks and the sound reverberated through the attic. There was no way that *they* would not know what he was doing. For the longest time he sat there, rubbing his raw, bleeding wrists, not making a sound, his heart pounding in his chest as he waited for claws to tear him open.

But amazingly, that didn't happen.

He knew the vampires were in the darkness with him. Why didn't they go after him? Were they sluggish from their feedings? Was it some sort of game? Did it excite them to let him think he might get away only to attack him at the last moment?

He waited a few minutes.

Sweat ran down his face and his nose wrinkled at the smell of death all around him. The stink of putrefied flesh and corpses rotting green. He knew that some of it must have been from their victims, but much of it was the way they smelled—not just putrescence, but a wild, gamey odor that was their natural scent.

He could see the broken roof overhead, the gaping holes in it. Whatever this place was, it was old and rotting, probably ready to fall down. The moonlight that spilled in provided him with an illuminated path that led for maybe fifteen feet over warped planks.

Drake was nearby. He knew that much. Not that it mattered because he was insane now. His mind was too far gone to bother with. In the end, Gus supposed, Drake had gotten exactly what he'd deserved. He felt no pity for him. In fact, at that moment, geared into survival mode, pity was a concept that was completely alien to him.

Breathing deeply and slowly to calm himself, he began to move. He did not get up: he crawled on his hands and knees down his moonlit path. Something crawled over his forearm and he flicked it away. His face broke through nets of cobweb. He heard a fluttering of vast wings and instinctively pulled into the darkness. Something bumped his head and then bumped it again.

He nearly screamed.

He had to clench his jaws tightly to avoid doing so. He couldn't see what was above him clearly. It was just a shape. He reached up and touched a boot. There was a man hanging there as he suspected. He moved down a few feet more and saw another shape above him and touched another boot. A drop of blood dripped from the body and broke against his cheek.

Despite the terror that filled him and the repulsion he felt, he moved farther down and found two more hanging bodies. He had no idea how many there might be. They were strung up like carcasses in a slaughterhouse and no doubt for the same reason, save they were alive. Living blood donors for the vampires.

He kept crawling, following his path of light, but staying in the shadows. He heard one of the men above him whimpering. He heard another praying in a broken voice.

*There's nothing I can do,* he told himself. *Nothing at all.*

He crawled forward and put his hand in something soft. It felt like congealed pudding. The sickly-sweet stench of decay blew into his face, hot and nauseating. Oh Jesus, it was the remains of a corpse, one in an advanced state of putrefaction, rotted to a human mulch, a soup of bones and stewed flesh.

*Gah.*

He gagged, but held it in. He had to be strong now. Stronger than he'd ever been in his life and stronger than he could imagine. He circled around the corpse, noticing with bile rising into his throat that his hands were sticky from its drainage on the floorboards and that the knees of his stripes were adhering to it. They sounded like masking tape being pulled free every time he lifted one.

His outstretched hands found what might have been a few stray bones and then something else. It was long, metal, and cylindrical. A flashlight. A cop's flashlight. One of the lights the guards used at night as they walked the corridors of Stackhouse, shining them into cells to make sure the cons were indeed sleeping.

Christ, now that was something.

But did he dare use it?

He made himself calm down. He had to think. He had to reason. He had to be very careful now. He found it very hard to believe that the vampires did not know what he was doing. They must have been able to see in the dark. That would only make sense. And if they could do that, then it was pointless to hide from them. If one of the guards had dropped a flashlight then there was a good possibility one of them might still have a gun on him.

He reached up and touched another boot. But just by the feel of it he knew it was not a boot, but a shoe. One of the cheap shoes the cons made in the cobbler shop. He backtracked, moving around the rotten corpse and reaching up. A guard's boot. No mistaking it. Setting the flashlight down, he got up on his knees, tracing his hands up the man's legs until he reached his holster.

Empty.

He tried another.

Empty.

Then he came to the man that was praying. As soon as he touched him, he began making a pathetic whining sound in his throat. *"Help me ... oh please, somebody help me..."*

But Gus knew he had to turn his heart hard if he wanted to get out of this. The chances of survival were miniscule as it was. So, he found the guard's gun belt and his heart jumped because the pistol was still in there. He popped the catch and slid the .38 into his pocket.

*I'm sorry, God knows I'm sorry.*

Down to the floor again, following the path of light. Around the corpse. And again, he wondered: *Why aren't they stopping me?* Hadn't he read once that fate favors the daring? He was back where he had been now, where he found the flashlight. Again, did he dare use it? He didn't think he had much of a choice. The .38 in his right hand and the flashlight in his left, he turned it on. The first thing he saw was a guard slumped in the corner. His eyes were wide and staring, his throat torn out. Clotted blood wound around his neck like a scarf.

He was dead.

Gus brought the light around and illuminated what was on the other side of the attic room. His heart galloped to a stop and he nearly fell over. Blood rushed into his limbs and then into his head.

On the floor were the remains of at least six or seven horrifically decomposed bodies, most of which looked like mummies. They were threaded with cobwebs, eye sockets empty, skulls covered by a thin veneer of cracking yellow flesh. But a few were more recent, maggoty things covered in flies, decaying into a communal sludge of flesh, blood, guano, and nameless putrescence.

Above them were three vampires.

They hung from the rafters above by clawed feet like bats in a cave. They were roughly the size of men; skeletal, gaunt things with gray-brown flesh set with irregular wiry tufts of fur. Folded-up wings were wrapped around them like cerements, their triple claws hanging downward. One of them flinched at the intrusion of light, spreading out a five or six-foot wing, the skin drawn tight and sheer between bony struts. It made a guttural, growling sound, its high pointed ears trembling, mouth yawning and long yellow fangs, uppers and lowers, scraping together like knife blades. Its eyes were pink and staring, catatonic-looking.

Gus just sat there on his knees, unable to pull the beam of light off of them. His arm seemed frozen in place. They seemed to be resting, sleeping, dormant or something.

He finally turned the light away, his skin crawling at the idea of being in the dark with them. The very sight—and stink—of them awoke some primal loathing at his core. But the light showed him that there was an archway at the end, another room beyond.

Carefully, he moved his way down there and saw that much of the roof was missing here, too. There were no hanging bodies. There was something much worse—crude wooden crates, coffin-sized boxes, seven or eight of them. Old, splintered things, water-stained, the lids spread with black whorls of mold.

But there was a doorway down there.

To get to it would mean moving amongst the boxes. The very idea terrified him, but he knew there was no other way. His mouth was dry, his belly rippling with slow, peristaltic waves that seemed to move through his chest and up to his throat. The utter fear that owned him was both physical and psychological and perhaps even spiritual. He had gone through a sort of awakening, a conversion, where he now believed in things that rational minds dismissed. He believed in vampires ... at least, the subhuman horrors that inspired their legends. He also believed in evil. It spawned and grew here as naturally as fungi beneath a rotting log. He knew its smell, its feel, the way it seeped into you and turned your mind soft and brown as a rotten apple.

*You can't go forward and you can't go back.*

He stepped forward, weaving amongst the ancient crates, his stomach quite literally in the back of his throat and his legs filled with rubber. The doorway was just ahead. He could do this. He could really do it. The door wasn't far; twenty-feet at the most.

Swallowing down the fear that gestated in his belly, ever aware of what was sleeping in the room he had just left, he moved toward the crates. The anxiety inside him was like razors peeling back his determination and willpower in fatty pink seams. His breath seemed to catch in his throat. He heard the squeaking of bats in his head and a mocking, cold laughter echoed in his skull.

There were things in those crates, he knew. Malevolent night-hunters that would drain him dry and swim in lakes of his hot, red blood. He could hear them breathing with low, rasping sounds.

*Focus. Get to that door.*

He moved silently amongst them, the .38 and flashlight shaking in his fists. A smell of corruption, nitrous age, and subterranean tombs issued from the crates. Graveyard fungi had grown over the lids in webs of filagree. Some morbid pink seepage had spilled from beneath the lids, slopping down the sides of the boxes and coagulating on the floor in mephitic pools. A rat ran across the toe of his shoe and he nearly screamed. It was bloated from its charnel feastings upon the vampires' many victims.

Finally, he reached the door just as something shifted in one of the boxes like a corpse rolling over in its grave. Sweat that was cold and oily rolled down his forehead and dripped from the tip of his nose.

Pocketing the .38, he gripped the doorknob.

It was thick with grime, but surprisingly, it moved freely. Still, the door would not open. It was warped by age and dry rot, swollen in its frame. He knew he could easily force it, but the noise … God, it would have been like a bomb going off.

Behind him, there was the worst possible of sounds: a low creaking.

Not like a door in an old movie, but a loud, pained noise like nails being pulled from an ancient plank. He fumbled in his pocket for the .38 and it slipped from his sweaty palm, dropping to his feet.

He saw one of the lids rising, gripped by a triple set of long, chitinous claws like yellowed ivory. Gooey, glistening strands of slime connected the lid to the box, each of them separating and dribbling down the side.

He gasped and nearly fainted.

A vampire inside the crate fixed him with beady, blood-drenched eyes set in deep, dark sockets. The triangular skull-like hollow of its nose wrinkled as if it was smelling him. Its face was gray-green, obtrusively bony with jutting knobs of bone and sunken hollows. The taut, flaking skin was seamed and beaded, somehow reptilian, yet still blatantly bat-like. Its jaws widened into a sardonic grin, black split lips curling away from pale gums and huge discolored fangs, the canines of which were practically tusks.

It made a low feral snarling sound, saliva hanging from its mouth in white, foaming ribbons like that of a rabid dog.

It gazed on him with unearthly wrath.

Terror flooded him. It seemed to ooze from his pores as his stomach tied itself in knots and fingers of white heat spread through his chest. He made an involuntary moaning sound that was infantile and high-pitched. Urine ran hotly down the inside of one leg of his stripes.

The vampire just watched him.

Some lost, distant part of his brain, said, *the gun, the gun, Jesus Christ, pick up the gun while you still can,* but it seemed to come from some infinite point in time and space.

The vampire lifted both of its taloned paws upwards, stretching the gossamer hide of its wings with a rubbery noise. He saw its body—the thrusting bony cage of its ribs, the flesh pulled tight over the rungs of the alien skeleton beneath—and something more: rows of flaccid teats that reached from its chest to belly, the nipples like black pushpins.

A female.

It was a female.

And as that pearl of wisdom flared in his brain, she cocked her head as if hearing his thoughts … and for one disturbing moment he thought he could feel her mind crawling over the convolutions of his brain like an unclean, inching slug.

She leaned forward out of the box and he saw that there was a spiky black mane of hair atop her head like a mohawk. Her jaws closed, upper and lower canines interlocking, projecting up and down out of her mouth like the teeth of a crocodile.

When she opened them again, he thought she would howl at him with bestial rage, but she didn't. Instead, with a voice that was hissing, liquid, but definitely female in timbre, she said, *"Guuuuuuusssss…"*

And that's when he hit the floor, his eyes rolling back white, his mind jumping in and out of consciousness rapidly. The only thing he was aware of after that was her gripping his ankle and pulling him across the floor.

## -12-

When Mac reached the place where *they* waited, he knew it instinctively. He could feel it along the nape of his neck and right up his spine as if a spider was climbing his backbone.

"Here," he said in a low, wistful voice. "This is it. This is where they wait."

Underwood and Peters stopped.

"Hell, you talking about, Mac?" Underwood asked, dread beneath his words.

And Mac wanted to laugh out loud. Oh, dear sweet God and lord of all things, how he wanted to burst out laughing as he had never laughed before. He wanted the heavens to boom with his secret mirth and the world to shake because Underwood—old hand, clever old boy, good old Pop—didn't know a goddamn thing and he understood even less.

*I could tell you things, you cocky know-it-all sonofabitch! I could let you in on mysteries that would turn what's left of your hair whiter than the snow on Santa's fucking roof! Oh yes, oh yes, oh most certainly YES!!*

"Is this it, Mac?" Underwood said, unholstering his service revolver. "Is this where they told you to bring us? Is it, Mac? Is this the place you betray your own kind?"

Mac still wanted to laugh at him.

What did he know?

What did that old sonofabitch even know?

The three of them were standing on a dark spit of land that crossed through steamy bogs, floating mats of reeds and shaggy undergrowth. It was the sort of place where one wrong step and you'd be sucked up to your neck in black mud that would never let you go. Clouds of phosphorescent insects swarmed over the bubbling mire. Skeeters and gnats speckled faces and throats. Drifting plumes of swamp mist rose all around them like cemetery sheets.

"Call 'em, Mac," Underwood said. "Call 'em out of their waterlogged graves."

"What are you talking about? What the hell are you talking about?" Peters demanded, shaking so badly in the bright moonlight it looked like his skin might unravel.

"Get your gun out," Underwood told him. "Mac's made a deal with the Devil and brung us to the killing grounds."

There were things Mac could have said at that moment as he felt the atmosphere around them go positively noxious and his own mad and hysterical thoughts skittered about in his head like white mice. But he didn't speak—it felt like his lips were gummed shut.

And then the world exploded around them.

The bogs erupted with black water and runny brown mud. It sprayed up into the air and rained back down on the men like a sudden, violent summer squall.

And out of the water and fog, night-winged shapes burst free from the stagnant depths, swooping and veering, flapping and shaking water from themselves, soaring into the mist and out of it, leaving steaming contrails in their wake.

Mac hit the ground and Peters screamed as the vampires swarmed them from every conceivable direction. Underwood fired again and again. Then he stopped because he no longer had a hand to fire with—it was on the ground, still gripping his service revolver. At the end of his wrist there was only a stump, blood jetting from an open artery. He sank to his knees with a cry of horror and a night stalker leaped from the shadows, slashing open his face with its claws. His eyes were ripped from gored sockets. From the crown of his skull to his chin, he was split right open, a fountain of meat and blood spraying into the underbrush.

He tipped straight over like a post and two vampires leaped on his back, flensing him with their talons like the blubber of a whale. They yanked pink sheaths of muscle free and finally his spine itself.

Peters tried to run and claws and teeth laid him open with blinding velocity. He managed a gurgling cry as an ocean of blood exploded from his mouth. He made it two or three steps, clutching the fleshy hoses of his own intestines before pitching over, the vampires crowding him, a dozen sucking mouths vacuuming the blood greedily from his ruptured body.

Mac saw it all, his mind reduced to mucilage. He was spattered with blood and meat, only his wide, white eyes visible in his ensanguined face.

*"I brought them to you, didn't I? Didn't I?"* he stammered. *"Just like you wanted! I did it just like you wanted! Now you have them…now you have them…"*

At which point, he curled up in the grass, sobbing and sucking his thumb as he had in his crib so many years before. Winged shadows pranced around him as he alternately giggled and cried like a child, listening to the terrible sounds of the vampires feeding.

## -13-

Pegg led Teague and the others to the place they needed to go. The four of them stood there, staring out across a small, dark lake whose waters issued a dank, curling mist.

"This is it," he said.

But they didn't need to be told that: they could feel it. Out in the middle of the lake beyond the high reeds was a sort of small island with a house built on it. It was old, falling apart, a tall and narrow black structure leaning precariously to one side, planks hanging free, no glass in the multitude of windows, a series of sharp-peaked roofs capping it off. Who built it out here many, many years ago or why was a mystery, but they all could feel the evil seeping from its marrow, oozing down its crowded corridors, and dripping like sap from its windows.

A plank boardwalk, badly rotted, led through the reeds and across the water to its porch.

This was it.

They either went in there and took care of business or they ran far away as fast as they could.

"But they'll never allow it," Pegg said.

"Who?" Labonski asked.

"Who do you think?"

Marco looked from Pegg to Teague as if he was waiting for some common sense from either one of them and not getting it. "We could always wait for dawn, you know. Come back with fifty men and tear this place apart."

Pegg just shook his head. "They're not stupid, son. They have a plan same as we do. If we wait, they're going to fly off to another location to spend the day. I'm willing to bet that place has already been selected. But before they go, they're going to slaughter everyone they've taken. And it won't just be cons like Drake and Gus. They'll kill every one of them."

"And how do you know that?" Marco asked.

Pegg didn't bother explaining. It would have taken too long if he had to put into words what his gut suspected and what that other unknown sense confirmed.

"We're running out of time," he said. "I'm going in there. If you want to stay out here while your friends die, you go ahead."

With that, he stepped onto the boardwalk. It held him. He waited no more. It was time.

### -14-

They were four men going to their death and nothing less was acceptable if they wanted to call themselves human beings. Their suicidal bravado satisfied that urge for self-destruction that dwells in all human beings and satisfied their need to die for a reason. It's what made men go to war and run unacceptable risks.

The boardwalk creaked and moved as they walked on it, spaced out evenly because as they put their weight on it, it sunk two or three inches beneath the waterline. They didn't know what held it up from below and they didn't have time to find out. Dawn was coming. If they didn't get this done, a lot of people were going to die if they weren't dead already.

There was hesitation in Marco and Labonski, even in Teague to a certain degree, but not Pegg. To him, his entire misspent life had led to this very moment where he either made things right or he died trying.

And nothing was going to stop him from getting to Gus. *Nothing.*

The high, nodding reeds pushed in from both sides, rustling uneasily and scraping together. Pegg knew that at any moment, one of the vampires might leap out and slash open his throat. Still, he was determined.

They were about halfway down that crazy, zigzagging boardwalk when they heard a sharp scream reverberate through the still air. It was the sound of a man being tortured to death, suffering untold agony. It stopped them on the boardwalk … but only for a few seconds because now they had a reason to charge in there and Pegg knew damn well that it was the vampires' intention to motivate them thusly.

**140**

Marco was swearing under his breath.

"Keep your head," Teague told him.

Dawn couldn't have been more than an hour away. The moon had moved behind the trees now as it sank slowly in the western sky. Maybe they were too late.

Now there was another scream—from the same man or another, it was hard to say. It was a drawn-out screeching that echoed from the haunted house before them. It was cut off in mid-squeal as if its owner's tongue had been torn out by the roots. Then there came that sound they all knew so well by that point: the mocking, hollow, hyena-like laughter that rose and fell in eerie cycles before fading away entirely.

It was all so much like Pavuvu that Pegg seized up for a moment. It felt like he was in the war again and maybe he was at that.

Now the house was right before them, huge and dark and sepulchral. Its front door was hanging by one hinge, sprung like the lid of a coffin.

Pegg led the way in.

## -15-

Inside the house, there was about three inches of water on the floors which were soft with rot. Teague stepped carefully. They were in a sort of wide foyer, panning their lights about over bowed walls and a drooping, water-stained ceiling. Nets of cobwebs were festooned in the corners, great ulcer-like holes rotted through the ancient paneling.

"Upstairs," Pegg said.

Teague nodded, moving forward, splashing through the standing water. Things floated in it—dead leaves, sticks, the shriveled bodies of dead rats. This was a place of death, a mortuary, and he could feel the ancient evil dripping from the walls like poison.

He noticed with a twinge of revulsion that there was dirt on the steps leading to the second floor. Great black clods of it, worms squirming in it, beetles the size of cigar butts crawling through it.

Pegg started up, the stairs creaking loudly. It would be a miracle if they held. He had his .30-06 in one hand and a flashlight in the other.

The light made shadows bunch and slither along the staircase walls, creating distorted, grotesque shapes in constant sweeping motion.

Another scream.

This one very close.

The vampires were beginning their slaughter, trying to urge the men to rush up the stairs blindly and recklessly where they'd be waiting for them. Waiting to kill them because, ultimately, that's what this was about, drawing them to their deaths.

There was a thudding noise above as if a body had been slammed against the wall. This was followed by a wet, fleshy tearing and the sound of splattering. Then a body came flying down the stairs, thumping end over end. Teague and the others pulled away at the last moment and it went past them, splashing into the water. It floated there, arms spread out, one leg twisted in its socket. It was a guard from Stackhouse; that much was obvious. Other than that, they couldn't say because it didn't have a head.

On the landing above, Teague caught a quick glimpse of a moving shadow and fired at it. Whether he hit it or not was anyone's guess.

Pegg did not fire.

He was very disciplined as he had been in the war and he wasn't wasting bullets until he had a real target.

"Let's go," he said, charging up the stairs without hesitation.

### -16-

The corridor above was long and narrow, the floor warped, the walls seeming to press in as if they were in a tunnel. Strips of faded, ancient wallpaper like sloughed skin hung down over ragged, rotted chasms. Water dripped. Rats skittered.

It was a slaughterhouse up there. Bodies, and parts of them, were scattered over the floors. Bloodstains sprayed over the walls.

"Oh Jesus," Marco said.

There were the remains of at least five bodies in the hallway, some little more than bones—a grinning skull, a femur or two, shattered spinal vertebrae, a crushed ribcage—but others were more recent kills: torsos and heads and limbs bloated with gas and writhing with maggots and black clouds of flies. They appeared to be lined up. Even the dismembered arms had their hands carefully clutched together, fingers interlaced as they would be at a funeral. The legs were arranged by size, heads in rows, blackened, puffy faces seeming to smile with the rictuses of death.

Pegg saw a long white worm exit an eye socket.

Then they were in the thick of it, stepping over the corpses and their parts, careful not to step on anything that would gush drainage and increase that stench of decomposition that hung in the air in gaseous clouds. Their light beams were filled with angry buzzing meat flies and drifting specks of dust.

And it was then, as they were boxed in, making for the doorway at the end, that Pegg felt it: *they were coming.* The vampires were coming. This was what they had been waiting for, this enclosed space where it would be nearly impossible for the men to shoot without hitting one another.

"Watch it," he said. "Goddammit, watch it now—"

Labonski let out a cry as a dark, flapping shape leaped through one of the holes in the walls. It jumped. It flew. It was among them. Overhead. Crawling up the walls like a bat. It was joined by another and another. Teeth were flashing, claws slashing out like the blades of scythes.

Marco lost control and started firing with his .38. Rounds punched into the walls, the ceiling. Pegg felt one of them pass by his left ear and he dropped to the floor, smushing a torso beneath him that ejected black slime like cream squirting from a squeezed pastry bag.

Teague shouted, feet slipping on the slime on the floor. He went on his ass as Labonski tried to jump away from two black shapes that vaulted at him. Marco emptied his pistol and screamed.

Labonski couldn't move fast enough. He tripped over some remains, smashed into the wall, turned and they were on him. Talons like the tines of a pitchfork punctured his stomach and he shrieked with agony. They were drawn upward with a powerful thrust and blood blossomed from his abdomen along with the hot stink of his own viscera.

It happened very quickly.

The claws slashed deeper and higher, catching his lower ribs and wetly snapping them like green sticks, his lungs perforated and wheezing, his entrails bursting from his cleaved belly with incredible, slopping force and spilling to the floor.

Teague shot the vampire in the throat with his .30-06, the impact nearly taking its head off. The next round went into the back of its skull which exploded in a gout of brains and skull matter, striking the wall like vomit.

It was absolute pandemonium.

Men screaming.

Vampires howling.

Guns firing.

Flashlight beams strobing in every which direction.

Teague tried to get off another shot, but it was impossible in the confines of the corridor. Labonski was still on his feet somehow, stumbling into the wall and dragging himself down its length, leaving a dark smear of blood. But his body blocked Marco who was seized by another of the vampires and lifted off his feet. It smashed him into the walls again and again, making the corridor seem to shake. With each powerful impact, things snapped and dislocated inside him. Blood exploded from his mouth and ass as he was he slammed mercilessly, reduced to a sloshing bag of liquid and shattered anatomy.

As he was tossed aside, Pegg killed the vampire with a perfect headshot that splashed its face right off the skull beneath, the impact throwing its carcass against the wall with such force it broke through, half of it hanging into the room on the other side.

The remaining vampire disappeared.

Or so it seemed.

As Teague climbed to his feet, ignoring Pegg who shouted for him to stay down, the missing vampire suddenly erupted right in front of him like a cloud of black ink ejected by a squid. It hit him with pulverizing velocity, knocking the rifle from his hands and sending his flashlight to the floor where it spun in circles.

He was lifted off his feet and crushed against the archway they'd just come through. His kidneys, liver, and lungs were smashed, his chest shattered, his guts forced up his throat with a cloud of blood and pushed out of his ass.

There was no surviving it.

He dropped to the floor, leaving a trail of gore down the wall. He flopped in his own blood and discharge for a moment or two before going still.

By then, Pegg had a clear shot of the vampire as it turned and launched itself through the air at him in a blur of speed. He fired his .30-06 in the scattered, spoking light, blowing a hole in its wing that made it crash to the floor, scattering body parts like a wave. He put the next one right in its ugly, snarling face, blowing its head into a confetti of flesh and bone.

Nothing moved in the corridor then.

Things cooled and stiffened, dripped and made popping sounds, but there was only death and flies and drifting smoke.

He was alone.

But he was far from finished.

## -17-

When he came out of it—whatever *it* was that drew his mind from his head—Gus knew instantly where he was. There was a phantasmal, half-memory of being hoisted into the air and dropped into a crate, the lid slamming shut.

The female's crate.

The smell in there was close, stagnant, and unbearably fetid, the air thin and gagging. He reached out his hands and felt dirt beneath him, damp soil that crawled with things. One of them crept over the back of his hand and another looped between his pinkie and ring finger.

*Bury you alive. She's going to bury you alive.*

A white-hot panic spread through him and he began to thrash and grind in the noisome dirt. Flies lit off his face, investigating his lips and his ears with an awful vibrating *zzzzzzt!*

His breath coming hard, his throat feeling dry and constricted, he forced himself to calm down. She wasn't going to let him suffocate—he was a tasty treat tucked away for later. And at a time of her own choosing, she would throw open the lid of his crypt and pluck him free like a caramel from a candy box. Then and only then would she drain his life-force, tonguing and sucking the sweet blood from him like the candied syrup from a chocolate-covered cherry.

As he controlled his breathing, he wondered how long he had until that happened. An hour? Minutes? Seconds?

He reached his hands up to test the lid and stuck them into something warm and pulsing. Slime oozed down his arms, droplets of it hitting his face. The black stench of it made his stomach contract and heave. Whatever it was—probably some sort of morbid fungus—it had grown all over the inside of the lid.

He would have to sink his hands through several inches of it to get any purchase on the lid itself.

That's when he heard a flurry of booming sounds somewhere in the distance that he knew were gunshots. Somebody was pouring out a serious volume of fire. It could have been guards from a search party, sheriff's deputies, or—

*Pegg! It's Pegg! He's come to get me out!*

He didn't know that to be a fact, of course, but he felt it to be true and his heart leaped with hope. Who else but that relentless, determined, tough son of a bee would even attempt an assault against a fortress of monsters?

*He loves you like you're his flesh and blood,* Gus thought. *You know he does. When hasn't he been there for you? Always ready with common sense and practical advice, a strong shoulder when you needed it and a ready fist when some animal crossed your path in lockup.*

It was around then that he became aware that he was not alone in the crate.

There was something in the dirt that was far worse than bugs or worms. He felt a sliding, boneless motion beneath his left leg. Then something similar under his back.

In the pitch blackness, he couldn't know what. They squirmed along his legs and one of them crawled against the bare skin of his forearm… something soft, nearly gelatinous that wriggled with fetal locomotion.

Another emerged between his legs and he did all he could do not to cry out. But he had to keep his nerve. He couldn't let Pegg down. Or himself. It paused at his crotch as if intrigued by the heat there. It tapped an appendage or maybe its head against his privates…then it relented, crawling onto his bare belly where his shirt was pulled up. It had a wormlike, larval form that was greasy with oily secretions. Tiny hairs or spines tickled his navel. It pulled itself forward, dragging its feverishly hot body with tiny claws that felt like pins piercing his skin. A scaly flap was drawn over his belly and he knew instinctively it was a rudimentary wing.

*The female,* he thought with rising horror. *It's one of her young, her spawn, her horrible progeny.*

Yes, they had burrowed into the black, moldering earth of the crate which she probably drenched with blood to nourish them. Now they had sensed him the way wasp larvae sense a venom-paralyzed spider in a hive. And like that drugged spider, they were going to feed on him.

That's why he was put here.

He seized the worming little vampire in his fists. It squirmed and fluttered its wings, tiny teeth biting into the thumb of his left hand. It made a low mewling sound.

Now what?

He had no weapons, not so much as a blade to cut it with … but he did have his strength.

It was exuding some kind of jelly, trying to lubricate itself so it could slip free.

Gritting his teeth, Gus bore down with everything he had until it squealed and he felt tiny bones popping inside it. He exerted more pressure until sweat beaded his face and the creature exploded in his hands, cold goo squirting between his fingers.

Another wriggled against his ankle.

He kicked it free and stomped it against the bottom of the crate.

A third nipped at his throat and he twisted it in his hands until something inside it snapped and more goo splashed over his fists.

He felt a few more burrow back into the soil. But he would get them. They were hungry and sooner or later he would crush the life from them.

### -18-

For some time, Mac crawled about through the endless dark distances of the Snakebit like a baby that had not yet learned the fine art of walking. After a while, still delirious, his mind gone soft as putty, he climbed to his feet like a toddler and walked, stumbling and directionless.

Drool ran down his chin and insects sucked the blood from his arms, neck, and his face which was grotesquely swollen with their bites. He kept running hands up and down his sweat-stained, badly torn uniform shirt. His badge winked like an eye. His fingers scraped away at crusty patches of blood and swamp mud.

A funny smell came off him that had little to do with what he had fouled himself with. It was a sour, glandular stink that what remained of his adult mind acquainted with raw fear.

*But you can't sweat fear,* a little voice told him. *You just can't.*

Though the idea did amuse him.

It made him giggle deep in his throat. But the laughter that eventually came from his mouth sounded like the whimpering of a strapped child.

*They'll come for me,* he thought.

*They'll come because I'm their friend and I did good things for them and they'll want to do good things for me.*

He looked to the sky which was dark, the stars just beginning to fade as dawn approached. He stumbled on, unaware of where he was going because his mind was no longer right and the stars—*oh, look at them!*—were so very beautiful twinkling above. He tripped over a root, slid in the grass, broke through a wall of dewy reeds, then fell into the swamp itself, legs sinking nearly up to his hips in the soft black mud, algae-slicked water rushing over his head.

He fought and strained, doing his best not to swallow any of the silty water, managing to work himself free. He fought to the surface, gasping for air. He clawed his way up into the reeds, crashing through them until he was on open ground again. He lay there, sobbing.

They were going to let him die out here.

They were—

He heard a flapping sound above him, then to the left and right. A freezing shadow fell over him. He shivered like a swimmer coming out of a cold lake.

He stood up.

They were all around him, standing there on stubby, hairy legs, their clawed feet splayed like those of hawks. They had their dark, bat-like wings spread out like Dracula's cloak. He could see the struts of bone and the thin veneer of flesh between them that looked no thicker than the skins of balloons.

He looked for understanding or compassion in their wicked faces, but what he saw was miles from that. Their eyes were succulent bright red cherries, their jaws hanging open, fangs jutting like knife blades.

He screamed, he begged, he offered them anything and everything, but in the end, one of them grabbed him by the throat and lifted him a full foot off the ground. As he gurgled with protestations, it brought its other paw up, talons fully extended, the tips of which were sharp as hypodermic needles. A quick, powerful upthrust of them and what was between his legs was ripped free. The claws not only emasculated him, but opened him up right to the throat, his stuffing falling out like the guts of a pinata.

They could have fed on him and made great sport of his death, but they did not. He was dropped to the ground, writhing and flopping in his own blood and bowels. He was worthless to them. He had betrayed his own kind and sooner or later, he would have betrayed them.

Maybe they didn't come to this conclusion as men or women would have, but they understood. Maybe it was the smell of his hormones and chemical emissions.

Regardless, they wanted no part of him.

When Mac stopped moving, they flew off, riding the high night winds, chittering and disappearing in the great silence beyond.

## -19-

When Pegg kicked his way through the ramshackle attic door, she was waiting for him like a hungry cat waiting for a mouse to emerge from its hole. She fixed him with small eyes like glittering rubies beneath a skeletal arch of bone. She was wrapped in the sheer membranes of her wings and he could see the elaborate vein networking in them. So powerful, yet so delicate.

He had the .30-06 in his hands and he had one bullet left. That's all that stood before him and an agonizing, traumatic death.

That moment in which they stared at each other became elastic and seemingly endless. He could have lived a lifetime in it. He felt himself growing woozy and weak, the blood in his veins like cold sludge. The cruel, reptilian domination of her mind sank deeply into his psyche like the fangs of a rattlesnake. He could feel the cold venom she injected into his brain, how it slowed his thinking and dulled his reactions. He could hear her whispering in the back of his head with the pristine, innocent voice of a child: *"Paaaay-gah...Paaaay-gah..."* And that voice in its hypnotic persuasion made him want to drop his rifle, fall to his knees and expose his pulsing soft throat to the sweet kiss of her appetite.

And maybe he would have.

But someone stumbled through the archway at the far end of the room.

Pegg's heart jumped with joy believing it to be Gus, but it wasn't Gus—it was Drake. And that made his blood boil and cleared his head.

The vampire queen was no less angry at his untimely arrival. She let out a screeching, yowling inhuman cry of utter rage. Her fangs gnashed together like carving knives and she laid her high, pointed ears flat against her skull. She spread her wings and they snapped open like a wet raincoat. Like the last time he had seen her on Pavuvu, her torso was covered in her squeaking, rustling spawn...except that these were older, more developed, much like the one he had killed earlier that night.

She uttered a strident cry and the vampire young flew from her in a swarm, wheeling through the air in a black tempest. Pegg thought they would come for him, but they descended on Drake, fastening themselves to him and forcing him to the floor ... feeding, sucking away what blood he had left. The best he could manage was a weak whimpering noise as they covered him, wings flapping and teeth biting and tongues lapping up his blood.

It was then that Pegg saw that the sky through the huge, yawning holes in the roof had turned aquamarine blue and the attic was noticeably brighter.

The sun was rising.

The vampire queen snarled at him and he knew she remembered what he had done to her mate all those years before.

Her wings went up.

She leaped.

He fired.

Of all the important shots in his life, this one went wild and did little more than graze her shoulder. She jumped atop one of the many coffin-like crates between her and Pegg, then vaulted through the air with extended wings.

He swung the rifle at her and she batted it aside, nearly taking his arm out of its socket. He hit the floor, but was on his feet instantly. He pulled the .38 with one swift motion and got two shots off as she came at him. One round went through her belly and the other into her chest.

Then she freed the gun from his hand with a swipe of her claws, taking two fingers off in the process. There was another of those inexplicably drawn-out moments. As the pain of his missing fingers turned his hand numb and clouded his mind, he saw how beautiful she was. Feral and predacious and utterly evil by design, but deadly beautiful. From the spiky mane of shining blue-black hair atop her streamlined head to her vicious jaws, from her huge wings that glistened like oiled leather to the pink striations in her flesh rising from the hairless vulva between her legs to the rows of teats swollen with milk that inflated and deflated as she drew in ragged lungfuls of air.

He pulled the only weapon he had left which was his shank and she was on him.

He slashed her, splitting one of her teats and she answered in kind, slicing through his stripes and laying his chest open. By then, she took hold of him and tossed him nearly ten feet. When he tried to scramble away, she threw him up into the air. He crashed down onto one of the crates, his ankle cracking like a pistol shot.

Still, he did not lose his shank.

She sliced him open, his right bicep bulging from the wound and he plunged the shank into her. Her claws took his nose off and wrenched his left eye from its socket. He slit her throat with the shank and she tore his belly open, seizing him and sinking her fangs into his shoulder as he rammed the shank into her again and again. Bleeding and battered and in incredible agony, he refused to give in.

He sank the shank into her chest and she sheared his lips from his face with a slash of her claws. By then, she was bleeding profusely, too, filled with a mindless rage at what he dared do to her.

She threw him eight feet where he slammed against the wall and she flew at him, charging with incredible velocity and the power of an artillery shell. She hit him and drove him into the wall again, bones breaking inside him, but the strength of her attack and the weakness of the rotting wall made it collapse. Still locked in a deadly battle to the death, they plunged out into the rays of the rising sun.

The effect was instantaneous: as the light struck her, she sizzled like bacon on a hot griddle. She let out a shrieking cry of pure anguish, trying to throw him, but Pegg clung to her, still stabbing her as she flew higher into the sky, then skimming the surface of the lake, leaving a greasy smoking contrail in her wake.

And then he knew he had her as she burned and flaked apart in his hands. He dug his fingers into the gaping wounds of her chest, snapping rib slats aside until he gripped her frantically pounding heart in his fists, yanking it free from its sheath of muscle and mashing the organ to a pulp.

She let out a screeching, reverberating death cry and, together, they plunged into the black waters of the lake. Her flesh crackled and sputtered, popping and steaming and liquefying as he bled out and they sank slowly into the muddy depths of the lake.

## -20-

Unbeknownst to either of them, Gus saw their mutual end. He had kicked himself free of the crate just in time to see them break through the wall of the attic into the purifying rays of the sun.

He cried out.

But there was nothing he could do.

Pegg was gone.

He stood there for some time before the cavernous hole in the sloping wall of the attic, staring down at the surface of the lake, at the spreading ripples where they had submerged, plumes of steam still issuing from the water.

He stumbled down the steps and out into the world, moving down the boardwalk, refusing to think, refusing to remember or even try to put it all into any kind of perspective.

He walked for many miles that long day until he was spotted and taken into custody. And when he told his story, they didn't like it very much.

## -21-

By ten that morning, Despair Island in general and Stackhouse Correctional in particular were swarming with federal, state, and county police of every description. And with them had come the newspaper people and TV crews.

In her office, Warden Keafer smoked a cigarette with trembling fingers. She'd just gotten off the phone with her old ally Blowden, the Commissioner of the BOP. He was her ally no longer. She was now his sacrificial lamb.

"What now?" Deputy Warden Eagleton asked her.

She blew out a cloud of smoke. "Did I ever tell you about the hamburger stand my father has in Cleveland? Oh, it's really something. He has a special recipe for big, juicy burgers. And once you have one, you'll never want another burger again. They're that good." She cleared her throat. "He has his stand set up in the industrial sector, factories as far as the eye can see. He employs eight people and sells over four hundred burgers a day, baskets of fries, countless Cokes and malts. He runs it from April to October and lounges about in Florida the rest of the year. He makes big money those six months he's open."

"And why are you telling me this?"

"Because my dad is retiring after forty years and I'm going to take over his operation. I'll bust my ass six months a year and lounge the other six."

"So you're quitting?"

She laughed. "Within the next forty-eight hours they'll demand my resignation and they'll get it."

He sat down. "But you had such great ideas, such great plans."

"I'm a woman in a man's world. Remember that. If any of this had happened to a man, they'd overlook it. But I'm a woman and I have enemies in every direction. They want me out."

"You could fight."

"They'd destroy me. They've been waiting for the chance."

"What now?"

She butted her cigarette. "Now I have to face the press and explain how, in a single night, I managed to get one of my guards murdered, lose five escaped cons and eighteen men that were searching for them."

"And how are you going to explain that?"

She winked at him. "By doing what any man would do—lying my ass off."

With that, she went to face the music.

# About the Author

**TIM CURRAN** is the author of *Skin Medicine, Hive, Dead Sea, Resurrection, The Devil Next Door, Dead Sea Chronicles, Clownflesh,* and *Bad Girl in the Box*. His short stories have been collected in *Bone Marrow Stew* and *Zombie Pulp*. His novellas include "The Underdwelling," "The Corpse King," "Puppet Graveyard," and "Worm, and Blackout." His fiction has been translated into German, Japanese, Spanish, and Italian.

# About the Artist

Born in Pennsylvania, **MICHAEL SQUID** is a horror author and filmmaker whose work has appeared in a number of anthologies and podcasts. His passion for storytelling and visual arts has led him into the world of filmmaking, where he aims to bring a fresh and dark vision to audiences.

# NEVER MISS A BOOK YOU WANT!

Join the Weird House mailing list
for the latest news, releases, and special offers!

## Scan this code or visit:
https://www.weirdhousepress.com/subscribe/

Made in the USA
Monee, IL
13 May 2024

58355645R00100